The Place That Never Left

John Faulkner

Chapter 1 — The Markers

The settlement was built as if it had circled itself.

From the outer lanes you could walk inward by degrees—past gardens trimmed to the same patient height, past stones set in careful patterns, past the small public places where people paused as though pausing were part of the design—and eventually you would arrive at the centre.

It was not a grand centre. Nothing rose there. Nothing demanded attention. There was no tower, no monument, no carved warning for strangers.

There was only the source.

Most people called it that without thinking. Not because anyone had declared it the proper name, but because the word had settled into use the way some words do—quietly, without argument, passed from mouth to mouth until it sounded like the only sensible thing to call it.

Elias lived on the third ring, near the path that curved closest to the centre before bending away again. Close enough to hear the centre when the wind was right. Close enough to smell the dampness after rain. Close enough to know, with a kind of involuntary familiarity, when something in the square had shifted.

Close enough to never go there.

He woke before the first bell, as he always did, and lay still long enough to listen. Not to anything specific. Just to the day arriving. There were sounds—someone moving in the house next door, a latch lifted too early, a cart wheel on stone—small confirmations that the world was continuing in the same direction it had yesterday.

When he rose, the floor was cold. He moved quietly out of habit, not because anyone slept. The house was empty in a way that had become normal: cups neatly placed, blankets folded, everything where it belonged. The emptiness was not sad, exactly. It was simply there, a kind of clean space that did not ask to be filled.

He washed his hands, warmed water, drank without tasting much, and dressed in the same plain clothing he wore for work. Not a uniform—nothing in the settlement was called that—but an understood set of choices. Certain colours. Certain cuts. A kind of modesty that was not enforced and yet somehow everyone shared.

Outside, the air held the cool of the night. The sky was pale. The centre of the settlement lay in its usual place, unseen but present, like a thought you could not stop having.

Elias walked the perimeter route toward the municipal sheds. The path he took was one of the approved paths—clear of the centre markers, clear of the damp stones that slicked when rain came, clear of the low wall that separated ordinary daily movement from the space people approached only when needed.

As he walked, he passed a child crouched in the dust, drawing lines with a stick. The child's knees were dirty. The child did not look up until Elias was almost beside him.

"Morn," the child said, as if the morning belonged to him.

"Morn," Elias replied.

The child's stick paused. His eyes moved past Elias's shoulder.

"Is it true it can hurt you?" the child asked.

Elias knew what *it* meant. Children always meant the centre when they said it, even when they'd never seen it closely. The centre was a kind of magnet for questions.

He stopped, not wanting to rush the moment. He had learned, over time, that answering children quickly made them feel foolish for asking. Children stopped asking if they felt foolish too often.

"It can," Elias said. The statement came out cleanly, like something rehearsed.

"How?" the child asked.

Elias hesitated. Not because he didn't know the answer, but because he did.

The answers were many, and most of them were stories. Some were warnings framed as memories. Some were memories shaped to become warnings. There had been a time when people spoke of the centre with ordinary familiarity, but that time felt distant, nearly imagined, preserved only in fragments: a grandparent's tone when they said a particular phrase, an old song with a line that no longer made sense.

Now, the centre was approached as you might approach a wild animal that had once been tame.

"It's not the kind of thing you explain like a bruise," Elias said finally. "It's more... you can get too close the wrong way."

The child frowned. "What's the wrong way?"

Elias looked down at the lines in the dust. The child had drawn circles, one inside another, with a dot in the middle. The drawing was innocent and exact, the way children sometimes saw things more plainly than adults allowed themselves to.

"The wrong way," Elias said, "is without care."

3

The child considered this with his whole body.

"But why is care the thing that stops it?" the child asked.

A laugh almost rose in Elias—soft, surprised, not unkind. The question was too direct. It came too close to the centre of the matter without knowing it.

He did not laugh.

"Because that's what we know," Elias said instead.

The child went back to the drawing, dissatisfied but not defeated.

Elias continued walking, feeling the question follow him like a small pebble caught in a shoe.

Because that's what we know.

He reached the sheds and joined the others already gathering there. The work they did was ordinary work: maintenance, repair, distribution, the small tasks that kept a community from fraying. There were lists. There were schedules. There were days assigned to certain routes, weeks assigned to certain checks.

Elias was good at it. Not in a way that drew attention, but in a way that made things smoother for everyone else. Tools returned to the right hooks. Materials accounted for. Measurements taken carefully. Problems addressed before they became arguments.

People trusted Elias.

Trust in the settlement often meant: *This person will keep things from becoming complicated.*

He did not mind being trusted. It carried a quiet satisfaction. It also carried weight.

That morning's list included a route that curved nearer the centre than usual. Not into the square itself, but along the inner lane where the stonework changed slightly, where the drainage lines were older, where the soil held more dampness even on dry days.

Elias read the list twice, then folded it with the same neatness he folded everything.

The route was not forbidden. But it was close enough that it required a certain composure. It required care. There were protocols for entering the inner lanes, though no one called them protocols. There were things you did without thinking if you were responsible. Certain pauses. Certain checks. Certain ways of carrying your tools so they did not clatter.

He gathered what he needed, nodded to Bren, and set off alone.

The inner lane was quieter. The buildings were lower, older, worn down by years of weather and careful repair. Most of the homes near the centre were occupied by those who worked there—those assigned to manage the square, the records, the gatherings. Not priests. Not guardians. Just people with roles.

As Elias walked, the sounds of the outer rings faded. The air felt slightly cooler. It might have been imagination, or it might have been the stone.

The markers appeared ahead: a series of upright posts set into the ground, each with a simple etched line across the top. No words. No symbols. Just the line, repeated, like a shared understanding made physical.

Elias slowed as he approached.

Not out of fear exactly—fear was too big a word, too dramatic for something that had become routine. It was more like the way you slow near a cliff edge, even if you've walked that path a hundred times. Your body remembers something your mind doesn't need to explain.

He stopped at the markers, as required, and looked down at the earth beyond them. The stones on the other side were darker, smoother, arranged with a care that seemed different from the rest of the settlement. The path beyond curved around the centre, skirting the square without entering it.

Elias's task today did not require crossing the markers. His work lay along the edge of the inner lane, where water sometimes pooled. But he stood for an extra moment anyway, as if waiting for something to confirm he was doing it right.

No one was watching.

And yet the pause mattered.

He turned away and continued along the permitted curve.

It was strange, how much of life could be built on small pauses.

The drainage channel he needed to check ran parallel to the marker line, close enough that Elias could see the square through gaps in the old hedges. The centre itself was not clearly visible—not from here. It was more a suggestion: a widening of space, a change in the way the air moved, the sense of openness held back by careful design.

At one point the hedge thinned, and Elias caught a clearer glimpse of the square. The stone there was paler. The ground was clean, as if swept regularly, though no broom marks showed. In the middle, the source lay quiet, sunk into the earth the way a spring might be, ringed by stones worn by hands.

It looked smaller than it should have, given how much it occupied people's minds.

Elias felt something then—an impulse, small and surprising, like thirst.

Not for water.

For closeness.

He swallowed, as if swallowing would settle it, and bent back over the drainage line. The channel was partially clogged with leaves. He cleared it carefully, using the tool he carried for such work, and watched the water begin to move again.

As it moved, he became aware of his own body in a sharper way: the tension in his shoulders, the tightness between his ribs. The way his jaw held itself even when no one spoke to him.

He paused, tool in hand, and tried to loosen it.

The looseness did not come easily. It felt like trying to relax a muscle you had forgotten you owned.

A voice sounded behind him—soft, not startling.

"You're early."

Elias turned.

Maren stood a few paces away, not close enough to intrude, not far enough to ignore. Her hair was grey at the temples. Her hands were clean. Her posture was careful in the way of someone who did not want to be a threat.

Maren belonged to those who oversaw the centre—who kept the records, the histories, the careful explanations that had gathered around the source over time. She rarely invoked that authority. Her presence alone usually carried enough weight.

"I had a long list," Elias said.

Maren nodded, eyes on the drainage channel. "It's good you're checking this before it backs up again."

Elias waited.

"It's quiet today," Maren said, after a moment.

"It is," Elias replied.

They stood there together.

"Sometimes people forget the markers are there for a reason," Maren said gently.

"I haven't crossed them," Elias said, keeping his tone even.

"I know," she said quickly. "I didn't mean—" She paused. "Only that familiarity can make us careless."

Elias nodded. "I'm careful."

"I know you are," Maren said.

There was relief in her voice. And something else—something like gratitude.

"Will you be at the gathering tonight?" she asked.

"Yes," Elias said. "If I finish the route."

"You will," Maren said, as if it were not a hope but a fact.

She stepped back, leaving him to his work.

Elias watched her go, then returned his attention to the water now moving freely through the channel.

It ran without drama, doing what water did when given space.

Later, as he walked home in the rain, the settlement looked as it always had.

And yet something in him felt close to a door he had never tried to open.

He slept deeply that night.

Chapter 2 — The Gathering

By the time Elias reached the inner lanes, the rain had thinned into a fine mist that clung to hair and cloth without ever falling in drops. The lamps along the path had already been lit, their light shallow and steady, not meant to brighten the world so much as to mark it.

People were moving inward from the rings in small groups, carrying dishes wrapped in cloth, carrying stools, carrying children whose shoes had been lost to puddles and retrieved again. Their voices stayed low. Not solemn—just contained, as if the space near the centre made everyone slightly more careful with sound.

The gathering was not held in the square itself. It never was. It took place at the edge of it, where the stonework widened into a shared courtyard, sheltered by an overhang supported by old beams. From there you could see the markers clearly, and beyond them the pale stones that circled the centre like a thought kept at the edge of speech.

Elias arrived with his hands empty. He did not need to bring anything. People had long ago stopped expecting him to contribute food. He contributed in other ways. He was the one who fixed the broken hinge on the storehouse door before winter. The one who noticed the cracks in the outer wall before water got in. The one who carried quiet problems away before they became public ones.

He stepped into the courtyard and felt, as he always did, the slight shift in his body. A tightening that arrived without permission. Not fear exactly. The word was too sharp, too dramatic for what this was. It was the way you adjusted your posture in a room that mattered.

He found a place near one of the beams, where he could lean without looking like he needed support. Around him, people settled. A woman spread a cloth on the ground and arranged bread on it with deliberate care. An older man wiped his hands on his coat as if cleanliness could be achieved by effort alone. Two teenagers stood near the edge, whispering and laughing, then stopping abruptly when an elder passed.

The elders moved through the gathering with the same unhurried pace the settlement valued, greeting people, receiving dishes, nodding at children. Their calm was part of the architecture.

Maren was there, speaking quietly with someone near the front. Elias saw her glance in his direction once, briefly, as if counting him present. Her expression did not change, but something in the glance suggested she had been waiting.

He looked away before it could become anything.

The meeting began the way it always did: with small announcements, with practical needs named and assigned. A roof tile had slipped on the fourth ring. The grain stores needed shifting to the drier shelves. A child's fever had broken. Someone's cart axle had snapped and would need repair before market day.

It was ordinary. It was good. Elias listened, nodded when he should, and tried to let his shoulders settle.

Then a pause arrived—the subtle kind, the kind that doesn't announce itself but changes the air.

Bren stepped forward, holding a folded sheet of paper. He cleared his throat once, though his throat did not seem to need it.

"One more thing," Bren said.

People looked up. A few heads tilted. Children stilled.

"We'll be checking the inner drainage lines again this week," Bren continued, eyes scanning faces without landing on any. "The rain has been steady, and the ground near the markers has softened.

If anyone has work that takes them near the centre, do it with care."

The phrase landed softly. It was not a warning. It was a reminder. The kind adults accepted without question because reminders were safer than explanations.

Elias felt something in him tighten anyway.

Across the courtyard, a small voice cut through the quiet.

"What happens if you don't?"

Heads turned.

Lio stood near his mother's leg, half-hidden, half-proud of being seen. His hair was still damp from the mist. His face held no defiance, only the clean insistence of curiosity.

Bren blinked. A flicker of discomfort crossed his face—not annoyance, more like uncertainty. He glanced at the elders as if to see who would answer.

The Interpreter, Silas, was seated near the front. Elias had not noticed him until now. Silas rarely spoke first. He waited. He listened. He let words gather before offering them, as though language were something to handle carefully.

Silas looked at Lio with a mild expression that might have been kindness.

"It isn't about punishment," Silas said. His voice carried easily without raising itself. "It's about wisdom."

Lio stared at him, unconvinced.

"But what happens?" the child asked again.

A hush deepened, not because the question was forbidden, but because it reached for something everyone had learned not to touch.

Silas smiled slightly, a small easing of the mouth meant to soften the moment.

"Sometimes," he said, "people get overwhelmed. Sometimes they misunderstand what they're near. Sometimes closeness makes them reckless."

Lio frowned. "Why?"

Silas paused, and Elias watched him do what he always did: choose words that would keep the shape of the world intact.

"Because not everything is meant to be approached without preparation," Silas said.

A few people nodded, grateful. The answer sounded right. It sounded like the kind of answer you could build a life around.

Lio opened his mouth again, but his mother's hand pressed lightly against his shoulder—gentle, not scolding. The child subsided, still dissatisfied.

The meeting moved on. People released a breath they didn't know they'd been holding. The ordinary announcements resumed, and the sense of calm returned.

But something had shifted, and Elias could feel it.

The question had not been answered. It had been managed.

When the meeting ended, people stood and began to eat. They moved into clusters as naturally as water finding familiar channels. Elias remained where he was for a moment, watching.

He saw Maren speaking with an older woman, her hands folded, her head inclined as if she were listening to something heavy. He saw Silas rise and greet a group of men near the front, his posture open, his smile precise. He saw children dart between legs, receiving scraps of bread and pieces of fruit. He saw the markers beyond the courtyard, their etched lines pale in the lamplight.

The place that never left lay just beyond them, unseen, but not absent.

A small hand tugged at Elias's coat.

He looked down.

Lio stood there, holding a piece of bread in one hand, his other hand empty and somehow insistent. His eyes were wide, not frightened, not reverent—simply present.

"You said it can hurt you," Lio said.

Elias's mouth went dry.

"I did," he replied.

"And you said it's about care," Lio said.

Elias stared at the child. The boy's face was earnest in the way only children could be earnest—without performance, without strategy.

Elias said nothing.

Lio tilted his head slightly, studying him as though Elias were part of the question.

"Do you think it's true?" the child asked.

The answer Elias could give—the approved answer—rose easily to his tongue. It would have been simple to say yes. It would have ended the moment cleanly. It would have restored order.

But the memory of the inner lane returned: the pale stone, the quiet openness, the impulse like thirst.

He looked past the child toward the markers.

"I think," Elias said slowly, "that we've been careful for a long time."

Lio watched him, waiting for the rest.

Elias felt, very faintly, the pull to say more.

He resisted it.

Not because he was hiding truth. Because he didn't yet trust his words.

Lio's brows knit together. "That's not an answer," he said, not accusing, simply naming it.

Elias almost smiled. "No," he agreed. "It isn't."

The child took a bite of bread and chewed thoughtfully, as if considering whether answers were necessary. Then he wiped his hand on his shirt and did something that made Elias's chest tighten.

He pointed toward the markers.

"I could go," Lio said.

Elias's body reacted before his mind did. He reached out and placed a hand lightly on the child's shoulder.

"No," he said, too quickly.

Lio looked up at him. "Why not?"

Elias removed his hand as if it had burned him. He kept his voice steady.

"Because you don't go there alone," he said.

"But you could come," Lio said.

Elias felt the eyes of the gathering nearby—not watching directly, but aware. People became aware of movement near the centre the way birds became aware of a shift in wind.

Elias crouched slightly so he was closer to the child's height.

"Not tonight," he said.

Lio's face held a brief flash of disappointment. Then, as children often did, he accepted the boundary without making it into a moral failure.

He nodded once and slipped away.

Elias stood again and watched him disappear into the crowd.

For a while, he ate quietly. He spoke when spoken to. He nodded at jokes and made small sounds of agreement at the right times. He tried to behave as though nothing in him had changed.

But he could feel the place beyond the markers the way you could feel the ocean even from inland—its presence not visible, not audible, but undeniable.

Later, when the gathering thinned and people began to drift back outward, Elias remained longer than he needed to. The mist had thickened again, turning the lamps into soft halos. The courtyard stones were damp and cold beneath his boots.

He found himself standing nearer the edge than usual.

Not over the markers. Not past them.

Just closer.

The distance felt like a line drawn in his own chest.

A figure appeared beside him, quiet as mist.

Maren.

She did not look at him right away. She looked toward the markers, as if the sight of them were simply part of the evening.

"You've been lingering," she said, gently enough that it could be interpreted as observation rather than correction.

"I'm not trying to," Elias replied.

Maren's eyes shifted to him. There was no accusation in her face, only something like concern.

"Sometimes," she said, "people linger when they're carrying something they can't name."

Elias swallowed.

"I'm fine," he said.

Maren's mouth softened. She did not argue. She did not press. She simply stood with him, letting the quiet exist without forcing it to become a conversation.

After a moment, she spoke again.

"I heard Lio," she said.

Elias's shoulders tightened. "He asks questions."

"He always has," Maren said. There was a faint affection in her voice. "Some questions are harmless. Some are heavy."

Elias looked toward the markers again.

"Do you think questions are dangerous?" he asked before he could stop himself.

Maren's gaze returned to the centre. Her expression remained calm, but something in it flickered—memory, perhaps.

"No," she said. "Not dangerous."

Elias waited.

Maren exhaled slowly. "But questions can lead people to places they aren't ready to be," she added.

Elias felt the familiar shape of the warning, softer than most, wrapped in care.

"And who decides readiness?" he asked.

The question left him like a stone slipping from a hand. He had not meant to throw it.

Maren turned to him then, fully.

Her eyes held something Elias had not expected: weariness. Not the weariness of age, but the weariness of someone who had been holding a line for a long time.

"We do," she said quietly. "We try to."

Elias heard the honesty in it, and it unsettled him more than any certainty would have.

He looked away.

Maren's voice softened further. "Elias," she said, and his name sounded different in her mouth—less like a label and more like a recognition. "Whatever you're feeling... don't let it rush you."

He almost laughed, but no humour came.

"I'm not rushing," he said.

Maren nodded once, as if believing him.

Then she did something that was almost imperceptible. She stepped back—not away from him, but away from the markers, giving him space in the direction he'd been unconsciously leaning.

It was a small gesture.

It was also an answer.

Maren touched his arm briefly—light, not possessive—and then she left, moving back into the dimness of the courtyard.

Elias remained.

The lamps hissed faintly. The mist softened the edges of the world. The markers stood where they always stood. The centre lay beyond them, unchanged.

The place that never left did not call to him.

It did not warn him away.

It simply remained.

Elias turned at last and began walking home.

He chose a path that curved one lane closer to the centre than usual, then another that curved closer still.

Not toward it.

Not yet.

But in the direction his body seemed to recognise before his mind would allow.

Behind him, the gathering dissolved into the rings like water returning to familiar channels.

Ahead of him, the settlement held its shape.

And somewhere within that shape, quiet and present, was the source.

Still there.

Chapter 3 — The Inner Lane

The next morning arrived without ceremony.

Elias woke before the bell again, not because he had slept lightly, but because his body had done something unfamiliar in the night: it had rested. The difference was subtle but unmistakable, like waking in a room where the air had been changed while you slept.

For a moment he lay still, waiting for the usual sense of readiness to arrive—the bracing, the quiet tightening that prepared him for the day.

It did not.

He frowned slightly, then dismissed the feeling as fatigue mislabelled as calm. The days had been long. The rain had lingered. Anyone would feel off after that.

He rose, dressed, and stepped outside.

The settlement looked the same. The lanes curved where they always had. The gardens held their careful shapes. The centre lay unseen but present, like a constant you didn't have to check to know it was there.

Nothing had changed.

And yet Elias found himself walking more slowly than usual, as if his body were refusing to hurry without being asked why.

At the sheds, Bren handed out the day's lists without comment. The paper felt damp at the edges.

"You're on the inner checks again," Bren said, already turning to the next person.

Elias glanced down.

The route traced the familiar curve near the centre, skirting the markers without crossing them. He had walked it dozens of times. He nodded once.

"Alright."

As he gathered his tools, he became aware of something else—his hands were steady. They usually were, but this steadiness felt different. Less deliberate. Less maintained.

He told himself he was imagining it.

The inner lane was quiet when he reached it, the rain having driven most people inward. The buildings there stood close to the ground, their stones darker with moisture, their windows small and recessed. The air carried the scent of wet earth and old wood.

Elias walked with the same care he always had, but the care felt lighter, less like obedience and more like attention.

He passed the first marker and slowed automatically, even though his path did not require him to stop. He noticed how his body responded before his thoughts did—the slight lift of the shoulders, the small intake of breath.

He let the breath go.

The response did not repeat itself.

This unsettled him.

He continued along the permitted curve, clearing small blockages, checking joints in the stonework, making notes where water had begun to undermine the channel. The work went quickly. His hands moved easily, as if they had been relieved of some invisible instruction.

At one point, voices drifted toward him from the other side of a hedge.

Two women stood near a doorway just out of sight, their words carried softly by the damp air.

"…not that it's dangerous," one of them was saying. "Just that some people aren't ready."

"Ready for what?" the other asked.

There was a pause. Elias could hear the uncertainty in it, the way people spoke when they sensed there was a right answer they had never been given clearly.

"For closeness," the first woman said finally.

Elias stopped working.

The phrase settled oddly in him.

Readiness had been used often enough around the centre, usually as a kindness. *You're not ready yet. It takes time. Better not to rush.* It was language that postponed rather than forbade, that delayed rather than denied.

It had always sounded reasonable.

He resumed his work, but the rhythm felt disrupted now, as if a stone had been placed in a channel that had flowed smoothly before.

What did readiness feel like?

He had never thought to ask.

As he worked, Elias became increasingly aware of his own body— not in pain, not in pleasure, just present in a way that made its habits visible. The way his jaw set when he approached the markers. The way his pace adjusted without thought. The way his eyes avoided lingering on the square through the hedge gaps, as if looking too long would count as a kind of trespass.

He noticed, too, how little any of this had ever been chosen.

It had simply been learned.

At the narrowest part of the lane, the path dipped slightly, and the stone changed colour where water had run often. Elias paused there, looking down at the damp earth. The rain had softened it. His boot pressed in and left a shallow mark.

For a moment—no more than that—he felt something rise in him.

Not fear.

Something like thirst.

The sensation startled him enough that he straightened immediately, stepping back onto firmer ground as if he had leaned too close to a flame.

He stood still, listening to his breath.

The feeling passed, leaving behind only confusion.

You're tired, he told himself. *That's all.*

He wrote a brief note on his list and moved on.

By the time he finished the route, the rain had eased again. The air felt lighter, as though the settlement were holding its breath between weather systems. Elias returned his tools and notes without comment.

On his way home, he took the long route around the third ring, passing the small square where children gathered when the ground was dry enough. Today only one child was there, tracing shapes in the damp dust with the toe of his boot.

Lio looked up when he saw Elias.

"Did you go near it again?" the boy asked, without preamble.

Elias stopped.

"Near what?"

Lio rolled his eyes with exaggerated patience. "The centre."

Elias considered his answer carefully.

"I worked the inner lane," he said.

"That's near," Lio replied.

"Yes," Elias said. "It is."

Lio studied him, head tilted, as if measuring something invisible.

"Do you feel different?" the boy asked.

Elias opened his mouth, then closed it again.

"I don't know," he said honestly.

Lio nodded, satisfied. "That's what my mum says when she's wrong."

Elias almost laughed. The sound caught in his chest and came out as a breath instead.

Lio pointed with his foot to the marks he had made in the ground—circles, uneven and overlapping.

"It's all closer than people think," he said, as if explaining something obvious.

Elias looked down at the drawing. The circles had no clear boundary between them. They bled into one another, lines crossing and recrossing until the centre was no more defined than the edges.

"Maybe," Elias said.

Lio shrugged and ran off, conversation complete.

Elias stood there longer than he needed to, staring at the marks in the dust until the rain softened them beyond recognition.

At home that evening, he found himself restless without knowing why. He ate without hunger, sat without reading, listened to the settlement settle around him. The familiar sounds felt distant, as if he were hearing them through a wall that had thinned.

He went to bed early, then lay awake longer than usual.

Not anxious.

Alert.

His mind returned, again and again, to the feeling on the inner lane—the brief thirst, the absence of fear where he expected it. He tried to frame it, to place it inside a familiar explanation, but every attempt slid off without catching.

Eventually he slept.

In his dreams, he walked the inner lane again, the rain falling steadily, the ground soft beneath his feet. In the dream, he did not slip.

He simply stood near the markers, feeling the pull of something unnamed, and did not know whether the danger he had been taught to fear was real—or only inherited.

He woke before the bell with the question still resting in his body.

Not sharp enough to demand an answer.

Not quiet enough to ignore.

And somewhere beneath it all, steady and unchanged, the centre remained where it always had been—close enough to be felt, distant enough to be avoided, waiting without urgency for whatever came next.

Chapter 4 — The Stories We Were Told

There were certain stories Elias did not remember learning.

They were simply there—settled into him like posture, like accent, like the way you learned to stand when someone older entered a room. No one ever gathered the children to explain them fully. They were absorbed instead, carried in tone and timing, in what was said and what was left unsaid.

The centre was one of those stories.

That morning, Elias found himself thinking about it not as a place, but as a narrative—something layered over time, added to carefully, generation by generation, until it felt solid enough to walk on.

He noticed this while repairing a latch on the outer storehouse door. The metal was old and had warped slightly with the damp. As he worked, an older man stood nearby, watching with the polite patience people gave Elias when he was fixing something.

"My grandfather used to say it was simpler once," the man said suddenly.

Elias paused, tool in hand. "Simpler how?"

The man shrugged. "Closer. People didn't fuss so much. Didn't need permission for every little thing."

"Why did it change?" Elias asked.

The man hesitated, as if surprised by the question.

"Well," he said slowly, "people realised you can't just trust everyone to know what they're doing."

Elias nodded, though something in the answer felt incomplete.

"Who realised?" he asked.

The man frowned. "I don't know. People."

The word landed heavily between them, as if it were meant to be sufficient.

They stood in silence for a moment longer, then the man cleared his throat and wandered off, conversation concluded.

Elias returned to the latch. It slid smoothly now, the door closing with a soft, satisfied sound.

People.

Later that day, Elias stopped by the records room to drop off a set of maintenance notes. The room was cool and dim, the shelves lined with bound volumes whose spines had faded into similar shades of brown and grey. The air smelled faintly of dust and old paper.

Silas was there, seated at a long table, reading.

He looked up as Elias entered, his expression open and neutral.

"Elias," he said. "You're early."

"I finished the route," Elias replied, setting the papers down.

Silas nodded and stacked them neatly, aligning the edges with care.

"You've been taking the inner lanes more often," Silas said, not accusing, simply noting.

"They're on the list," Elias said.

"Yes," Silas agreed. "They are."

Silas closed the book he had been reading, resting his hand on the cover as if to keep his place.

"Do you ever wonder," Silas asked mildly, "why the centre draws so much attention?"

Elias felt the question settle in his chest.

"People talk about it a lot," he said.

"They always have," Silas replied. "Even when they pretended not to."

Elias waited.

Silas leaned back slightly. "The earliest records don't describe the source as dangerous," he said. "Not in the way we think of danger now."

"What do they describe?" Elias asked.

Silas smiled faintly. "Unpredictable."

The word hung between them, ambiguous.

"That sounds like another way of saying dangerous," Elias said.

Silas tilted his head. "Sometimes," he said. "And sometimes it's another way of saying alive."

Elias felt again the sensation from the inner lane—the brief thirst, the absence of fear.

"Why did that change?" he asked.

Silas's gaze drifted toward the shelves, toward the accumulated weight of recorded memory.

"People like clarity," Silas said. "They like knowing where they stand. Over time, unpredictability becomes a liability."

"So stories changed," Elias said.

Silas considered this. "Stories refined," he said. "Clarified. Made safer."

"Safer for whom?" Elias asked.

Silas's eyes returned to him, calm and attentive.

"For everyone," he said.

Elias did not argue. He thanked Silas and left the room, carrying the question with him like an unfiled document.

That afternoon, the rain returned in earnest. Elias took shelter under an overhang near the third ring and watched people hurry past, heads down, coats pulled tight. The settlement moved as one body when weather demanded it, efficient and practiced.

Near the edge of the square, two elders stood speaking quietly. Elias recognised Maren's posture even from a distance—the way she leaned slightly forward when listening, as if drawing the other person out rather than pressing them back.

The other elder spoke animatedly, hands moving, concern evident even without words.

Elias could not hear what they said, but he could imagine it.

We must be careful.
People misunderstand.
We have a responsibility.

The phrases were familiar. They had shaped his life.

As he watched, a child darted too close to the markers, chasing a scrap of cloth blown loose by the wind. An elder reached out reflexively and caught the child's sleeve, guiding him back with a firm but gentle hand.

The child laughed, unbothered.

The elder did not.

Elias felt something tighten in his chest—not fear, but recognition.

That evening, as the rain eased and people emerged again, Elias found himself remembering stories he had heard as a child. Not official ones, not the kind written down, but the fragments shared in kitchens and on doorsteps.

Someone who had gone too close and "lost their balance."
Someone who had stayed too long and "changed."
Someone who had insisted the centre wasn't dangerous and later "regretted it."

The details were always vague. The outcomes never clear.

No one ever said what had actually happened.

Only that it had been a warning.

Elias realised then that the stories functioned less as history and more as fences. They did not need to be precise. They only needed to shape behaviour.

At home, he opened one of the old notebooks he kept for maintenance sketches and lists. Instead of writing, he stared at the blank page.

He thought of the source—not as it had been described, but as he had seen it from just beyond the markers. Quiet. Ordinary. Smaller than expected.

He thought of how nothing had happened.

Not because it was safe.

Not because it was dangerous.

Because it simply was.

Elias closed the notebook without writing anything.

That night, he dreamed of voices telling the same story in slightly different ways. Each voice believed it. Each voice meant well. Each voice added a small caution, a small clarification, a small adjustment meant to help.

By morning, the original shape of the story was impossible to find.

When Elias woke, the rain had stopped. The air was clear. The settlement lay open and calm beneath the early light.

The centre remained where it always had been.

And for the first time, Elias wondered whether the distance he had been taught to keep was not a response to danger—but to uncertainty.

The thought did not accuse.

It simply waited.

Chapter 5 — Care

The word followed Elias through the day.

Not spoken often. Not emphasised. Just present—woven into instructions, folded into reminders, carried lightly as though it were self-explanatory.

Take care on the stones.
Careful near the centre.
Better to be careful than sorry.

Care was never questioned. It was treated as a virtue that needed no defence.

That morning, Elias was asked to assist with a small repair near the eastern storage rooms, where the path narrowed before curving back toward the third ring. The work was simple: resetting a loose stone, checking the support beneath it. The kind of thing that kept people from stumbling.

He knelt and worked steadily, aware of footsteps approaching before he heard the voice.

"Careful there."

He looked up. A woman stood a few paces back, holding a basket against her hip. She smiled when she saw him look.

"I mean the edge," she added. "It gets slick when the rain comes again."

"I know," Elias said.

She nodded, satisfied, and moved on.

The exchange was ordinary. Friendly. Unremarkable.

And yet Elias felt the word linger after she left, as if it had been set down beside him.

Careful.

He reset the stone and pressed it firmly into place. It held. The path looked no different than it had before, except now it would not shift underfoot.

As he stood, Elias noticed how instinctively he scanned the space around him—not for danger, but for proximity. How near he was to the centre. How the path curved away before it became a question.

The habit had formed so early that it no longer felt like habit.

It felt like wisdom.

Later, as the day warmed and people moved more freely again, Elias walked a short stretch with Bren, carrying supplies back toward the sheds. They did not talk much. Bren was a man who preferred silence to speculation.

At one point Bren slowed, gesturing ahead where the path dipped slightly near the inner lanes.

"Watch your step," he said. "That spot catches people off guard."

Elias nodded.

"I've seen it," he said.

Bren hesitated, then added, "Better to avoid it altogether if you can."

"Why?" Elias asked.

Bren glanced at him, surprised.

"Why take the risk?" Bren replied. "There's another way around."

Elias looked at the path. The alternate route was longer, less direct, but well worn.

"That path's fine," Bren continued, already moving on. "Just takes more time."

Elias followed, the question echoing faintly behind them.

Why take the risk?

He could not remember a time when that question had not seemed sufficient.

In the afternoon, he passed Maren near the edge of the square. She was speaking with two younger elders, her voice low but firm. Elias did not intend to listen, but one phrase reached him clearly.

"…care without fear," Maren said.

The words caught.

Elias slowed, pretending to adjust the strap of his satchel.

"One doesn't cancel the other," Maren continued. "Care keeps us attentive. Fear distorts attention."

The younger elders nodded, though one of them looked unconvinced.

"And how do you tell the difference?" the other asked.

Maren paused.

"That," she said, "is learned."

Elias moved on before he could be noticed.

Care without fear.

The phrase unsettled him more than it should have.

He had always assumed they were the same thing.

That evening, as the settlement gathered itself inward again, Elias sat outside his house, watching the light fade. The air was cool, the stones drying after days of rain. Somewhere nearby, children played, their voices rising and falling without concern for where they stood.

Lio appeared at the edge of the lane, dragging a stick behind him. He stopped when he saw Elias.

"Did you know," Lio said, without greeting, "that they tell us not to run near the centre?"

Elias smiled faintly. "Yes."

"But they don't say why," Lio continued. "Just that we should be careful."

"Yes," Elias said again.

Lio frowned. "If you don't know why something is dangerous, how do you know how to be careful?"

Elias opened his mouth, then closed it.

"That's a good question," he said.

Lio seemed pleased. He sat down cross-legged on the stone, tapping the stick against the ground.

"My mum says care means thinking ahead," he said.

"That sounds right," Elias replied.

"But thinking ahead of what?" Lio asked.

Elias felt the now-familiar pause open inside him—the space where answers used to arrive easily.

"I think," he said slowly, "that sometimes care is about protecting people."

Lio nodded.

"And sometimes?" the boy prompted.

Elias looked toward the inner lanes, where the path curved out of sight before reaching the markers.

"And sometimes," he said, "it's about protecting stories."

Lio considered this, then shrugged.

"I like stories," he said. "But I don't like them when they tell me where I'm allowed to stand."

With that, he stood and wandered off, conversation complete.

Elias remained where he was.

The word *care* settled again in his thoughts—not as instruction, but as question.

He thought of how often it had been used to slow people down. To redirect them. To postpone curiosity indefinitely.

He thought of how little anyone had ever explained what would actually happen if care failed.

Only that it must not.

As night fell, the settlement grew quiet. Lamps glowed. Doors closed. The centre lay beyond sight, beyond sound, beyond immediate concern.

Elias went inside and prepared for sleep, but he did not feel the familiar tightening that usually accompanied the end of the day— the sense of having successfully navigated another set of boundaries.

Instead, there was only a mild unease.

Not fear.

Something closer to honesty.

He lay in the dark and thought of Maren's words.

Care without fear.

He did not yet know what that meant.

But for the first time, he suspected that care might not require distance.

The thought did not settle.

It did not need to.

Act One closed quietly around him, the way the settlement always did—carefully, deliberately, holding its shape.

And somewhere beneath that carefulness, unseen but present, something waited without impatience.

Chapter 6 — The Slip

It happens because of weather.

Not a storm. Not a drama. Just the kind of slow rain that softens the ground without announcing itself, turning stone darker and soil less certain.

For three days the settlement had moved under a low sky. People carried coats over their arms and forgot to put them on. Children came home damp and shining, as if the air had touched them differently. The outer lanes held puddles that reflected the lamps at night in broken pieces.

Near the centre the ground changed first.

The stones there were older. The soil between them was thinner. Water did not sit politely in shallow basins. It seeped. It moved. It found the weak places that careful design could not fully anticipate.

That afternoon Elias was alone on the inner route again.

He had finished the western drainage checks earlier than expected, then followed the channel line along the permitted curve, stopping where the earth sank a little and the stonework shifted. He carried a small satchel of tools and a folded sheet with his notes. The rain had thinned to mist, then returned as a steady soft fall that seemed to come from everywhere at once.

He should have turned back sooner.

The work did not require him to go this far. The list did not demand it. But water had been pooling near the marker line and someone would have to clear it eventually, and it was easier to do it now than to let it become a problem that would need five people and a meeting.

Elias had been the sort of person who solved problems before they announced themselves.

It was one of the reasons people trusted him.

He reached the spot where the drainage channel narrowed and the ground dipped. A cluster of leaves had gathered there, pressed down by rain until they formed a dark mat over the opening. Water slid around it rather than through it.

Elias crouched and set his satchel down carefully, away from the slick edge. He pulled out the hooked tool he used for clearing narrow channels and slid it under the leaf mat.

The leaves resisted, then gave way in a single wet sound. Water surged through with a quiet urgency, as if relieved to be allowed to move.

Elias watched it for a moment, then shifted his weight to stand.

His boot slid.

It was not sudden enough to feel like danger at first. It was the kind of slip that happens when you assume stone will behave like stone and forget that rain changes everything. His foot skated sideways, the sole finding slick moss where moss had no right to be, and his balance moved in a direction his body did not expect.

He reached out instinctively for the nearest stable thing.

There was nothing.

The drainage edge gave slightly under his other foot, the soil loosening, and before he could correct himself he stumbled forward, arm swinging, notes crumpling in his fist.

He did not fall hard. He did not hit his head. He did not crash into anything dramatic.

He simply stepped—one step, then another—past the marker line.

The first marker was to his left, close enough that he could see the pale etched line at the top. The second was behind him. He could have reached out and touched the wood.

He stopped.

For a moment, he waited for his body to tell him what to do next.

His body, for once, did not offer panic. It offered something else: stillness. A pause so complete it felt as if the rain itself had quieted.

Elias stood with his chest slightly heaving from the slip and the correction, and listened for the internal alarm that usually arrived near the centre—the tightening, the sense of being watched, the subtle shame of being too close.

Nothing arrived.

The absence of it was almost worse at first.

He looked down at his boots. Mud clung to the edges. The stones beneath him were darker than the stones on the permitted path, smoothed by years of managed use. The air smelled faintly of wet earth, clean in a way that made everything else in the settlement seem suddenly dry and overhandled.

He should step back.

He knew that.

He also knew, in the same clear way, that nothing had actually happened yet. No voice had spoken. No elder had appeared. No injury had been delivered as proof.

Only his own breath, and the rain.

Elias lifted his eyes.

The square lay ahead, partly visible through the thinning hedge—paler stone widening into a space that did not carry the same narrow instruction as the lanes. In the centre of that openness was the source, ringed by worn stones, quiet as a bowl set into the earth.

It looked ordinary.

Closer, it looked smaller than it had from the edge. Less like a thing that could harm you and more like a simple fact.

Elias felt, with the same surprising clarity as thirst, that he had never actually seen it.

He had looked at it before, from approved angles, from controlled distances, through the lens of language that told him what it meant before his eyes could decide. But he had never seen it like this—unmediated, without ceremony, without the subtle pressure of belonging.

The rain continued.

A drop slid from his hair to his cheek. He wiped it away with the back of his hand and realised his hand was shaking slightly—not with fear, but with the after-effect of the slip, the adrenaline of near-falling.

He took one careful step farther in.

Not toward the centre. Not directly. Just to firmer ground.

He stood again.

Nothing changed.

The rain did not thicken. The air did not darken. The settlement did not lean toward him with collective awareness.

43

For the first time in a long time, Elias noticed his own shoulders.

They were high.

Not because of the slip. Because of everything.

He tried to lower them. The effort felt strange, like speaking a language he had not used in years. His shoulders did not obey at once. They loosened by degrees, reluctantly, as if unsure whether it was safe to rest.

Elias exhaled.

It was a longer breath than he intended. A breath that sounded, in the quiet near the centre, like admission.

With it something else released—something he could not name. Not a thought. Not a belief.

A tension that had lived under the surface of his days like background noise.

The relief of its absence did not arrive as joy. It arrived as embarrassment.

He had been holding himself like that for so long.

He had believed it was normal.

He took another step, then stopped.

He did not want this to become a decision. He did not want to become someone who crossed markers.

He wanted only to understand what was happening to his body.

He crouched again, because crouching was a familiar posture for work and familiarity made him brave. He set the crumpled notes beside him and rested his hand on the stone nearest the edge of the square, not touching the source itself, just the worn ring around it—stone smoothed by hands over years, by careful approaches and regulated moments.

The stone was cold.

It did not pulse. It did not warm. It did not respond.

It simply remained what it was.

And still the rest persisted.

It did not ask him to become someone new.

It did not ask him to confess.

It did not ask anything at all.

Elias stayed crouched, rain wetting his sleeves, listening to the water moving in the channel behind him.

He expected at any moment to feel guilt rise—something rehearsed and familiar, a kind of inner correction.

What rose instead was a quiet grief.

Not sharp. Not dramatic. Just the recognition of a long, unnecessary labour.

He thought of the child, Lio, asking why care was the thing that stopped harm.

He thought of the way Silas spoke—smooth words arranged into a shape that kept the world stable.

He thought of Maren's caution, gentle but firm, like hands holding a shoulder back from a ledge.

Elias did not feel anger toward them.

He felt distance.

As if he had belonged to a story that was no longer quite the right size for the truth.

A sound came from the inner lane behind him.

Elias froze.

Footsteps, soft on wet stone.

He stood quickly, wiping his hand on his coat as if being seen touching the stone would carry consequence. His heart thudded once, hard, and then steadied.

The footsteps stopped.

Elias turned.

No one was there.

Only the hedge shifting slightly in the rain, the leaves trembling from wind, or perhaps from his own breath moving them as he turned.

He realised then how deeply he had expected to be watched.

Even when no one watched.

Elias looked back at the marker line.

It was close. A few steps. He could return easily. He could pretend the slip was only a slip, the kind of thing that left nothing behind but mud on boots and a crumpled page of notes.

But his body had already learned something, and bodies were difficult to convince once they had tasted rest.

He stepped back over the markers slowly, deliberately, as though leaving a room he had entered by accident and now understood differently.

On the permitted path the stone felt familiar underfoot.

The air felt the same.

The rain was the same rain.

Yet Elias's chest remained open in a way it had not been when he arrived. His jaw was looser. The inner hum of vigilance had lowered, as if someone had turned down a volume he had forgotten existed.

He picked up his satchel, smoothed his notes as best he could, and folded them again.

Then he stood for a moment at the marker line, looking at the square through the hedge gap.

It did not call to him.

It did not threaten.

It simply remained.

Elias turned and began walking back along the inner lane.

Halfway to the sheds he realised he was walking more slowly than usual. Not because he was tired, but because he was not rushing. The difference was subtle, like the difference between carrying something heavy and realising you have put it down.

When he reached the sheds the evening had already begun to settle. Lamps were being lit. Voices rose and fell in the ordinary way of people finishing their day.

Bren looked up when Elias entered, glanced at the damp mud on his boots, and nodded once.

"Drainage moving?" Bren asked.

"Yes," Elias said.

"Good," Bren replied, already turning back to his own list.

No one asked where Elias had been. No one noticed the marker line in the mud on the edge of his coat where his shoulder had brushed it. No one saw the slight difference in his face, because the difference was not yet visible.

Elias hung his tool on the hook and stood for a moment with his hands empty.

He could feel his own body as if it were new to him.

He left the sheds and walked home through the third ring, mist rising from the stones as the rain eased. Children ran past him laughing, their voices bright and careless. Someone called his name from a doorway and he lifted a hand in response.

He felt normal.

And he did not.

When Elias reached his house he removed his coat and set it on the chair by the window. Mud fell in small pieces onto the floor. He did not brush it away immediately. He stood and looked at it as if it belonged to a different story.

He washed his hands, warmed water, ate without hunger.

Then he sat on the edge of his bed and realised, with a quiet shock, that he was not braced.

He had not noticed how braced he had been until the bracing was gone.

Outside, the settlement held its shape. The centre remained where it had always been.

The place that never left did not arrive with fanfare.

It was simply there.

Elias lay down and slept as if his body had been waiting for permission for years.

In the night he did not dream of warnings.

He dreamt of water moving freely through a channel, and the sound of it was not urgent.

It was only life, going where it had always meant to go.

Chapter 7 — Nothing Happens

The next day unfolds as it always has.

The bell rings at its usual hour. Doors open. People move into the lanes with baskets and tools and conversations already halfway formed. The settlement wakes without ceremony, continuing the shape it learned long ago.

Nothing feels different.

And yet Elias notices everything.

He wakes before the bell, not abruptly, not with urgency, but as if his body has reached the end of rest on its own. He lies still for a moment, waiting for the familiar sense of assessment to arrive— the quiet internal inventory that asks whether he is ready, whether he has missed something, whether the day requires vigilance.

The questions do not come.

He sits up, surprised by the ease of it, and swings his legs over the edge of the bed. The floor is cold beneath his feet. The air smells faintly of damp stone and morning bread.

Ordinary.

He dresses, washes, eats.

Nothing happens.

Outside, the third ring is already stirring. A cart rattles past. Someone laughs too loudly, then lowers their voice without knowing why. A door closes with a sound that echoes briefly and then disappears.

Elias steps into the lane and feels his body move forward without bracing.

He almost stops.

The absence of tension is so noticeable it feels like a mistake.

He walks on.

At the sheds, Bren hands out lists. Their fingers brush briefly as the paper changes hands. Bren does not look at Elias differently. He does not pause. He does not ask questions.

"You're on the outer checks today," Bren says.

Elias nods.

He feels, unexpectedly, a flicker of disappointment.

The outer routes are straightforward. Safe. Well away from the centre. He has walked them so many times his feet could follow the curves without instruction.

He gathers his tools and sets out.

The work goes smoothly. Too smoothly.

Elias resets stones, clears debris, makes small repairs. His hands move with practiced ease, but something about the work feels lighter, as though it is no longer carrying an unspoken burden alongside the task itself.

He realises, midway through the morning, that he is breathing more deeply.

Not deliberately.

Not as an exercise.

Just breathing.

The thought makes him self-conscious, and he waits for the breath to tighten again, to resume its familiar shallow rhythm.

It does not.

Nothing happens.

He passes people he knows. They greet him as they always have. Their faces hold no alarm, no curiosity sharpened by rumor.

No one knows.

Or if they do, they do not say.

At midday, Elias eats in the shade of a low wall near the outer ring. The bread tastes the same. The water is cool. A sparrow hops near his feet, bold enough to approach, then retreats again.

The world continues.

He finds himself listening for something—for consequence, perhaps, or confirmation. A sense that what happened near the centre has registered somewhere beyond his own body.

There is none.

The settlement does not respond.

The absence of response unsettles him more than anger would have.

In the afternoon, a woman approaches him about a sticking gate near the market path. He follows her, tools in hand, and repairs it in a few minutes. She thanks him and moves on.

As he watches her go, Elias notices that his shoulders have remained low throughout the exchange.

He tries to remember the last time that was true.

Later, he passes near the inner lanes on his way home, not because his route requires it, but because the curve of the path brings him there naturally. He slows as he approaches the markers, then stops.

The posts stand as they always have. Pale lines etched at the top. Unremarkable. Firm.

He does not cross them.

He does not need to.

He stands there for a moment, rainless air brushing his face, and notices something quietly extraordinary.

The centre does not pull at him.

It does not demand explanation or repetition. It does not call him back to prove anything.

It simply remains.

Elias turns away.

At home, the afternoon stretches long and quiet. He sits by the window without opening a book. He watches people pass, their movements unremarkable and complete. He listens to the settlement breathe.

The stillness feels unfamiliar.

Not wrong.

Just new.

As evening approaches, the sense of waiting returns—not for an event, but for understanding. Elias realises he has spent most of his life assuming that meaning follows immediately on experience, that if something happens it must be named quickly or risk becoming dangerous.

This experience resists naming.

Every explanation he considers feels like an intrusion.

That night, he joins a small group for a meal. Conversation drifts easily, touching on weather, work, small plans for the coming days. Elias speaks when spoken to. No one presses him. No one watches him more closely than before.

Lio appears briefly, slipping between adults to steal a piece of bread. He catches Elias's eye and grins, then disappears again without comment.

Elias does not know whether the child senses anything.

He suspects children often do.

When he returns home, the lamps are already lit. The air is cool. The centre lies somewhere beyond sight, unchanged.

Elias prepares for sleep and lies down expecting restlessness.

Instead, sleep comes quickly.

In the night, he wakes once, briefly, and listens to the quiet.

Nothing is wrong.

Nothing is demanded.

Nothing happens.

And in that absence—in the lack of consequence, in the world's refusal to react—Elias begins to understand something without words:

Whatever he encountered near the centre did not require protection.

It did not need to be managed.

It did not need to be contained.

It was not fragile.

It would still be there tomorrow.

The thought does not comfort him.

It steadies him.

He sleeps again, deeper this time, and when morning comes, the bell rings as it always has.

The settlement wakes.

The centre remains.

And the most unsettling truth of all settles gently into Elias's body:

Nothing has happened.

And nothing ever needed to.

Chapter 8 — After

The change does not announce itself.

If Elias were asked later when it began, he would not know how to answer. There is no clear moment to point to, no line crossed, no decision made. Only a series of small recognitions that arrive too quietly to interrupt the day.

He notices it first in his hands.

They rest more easily at his sides when he walks. They no longer curl slightly inward, as if prepared to catch or correct something before it falls. When he reaches for a tool, the movement feels direct—less careful, more accurate.

The difference is subtle enough that he doubts it.

Subtle enough that he almost misses it.

At the sheds, Bren gives him a list and asks him to take a second set of tools along the inner lanes later in the day. The request is practical, not symbolic. Something near the drainage needs checking again after the rain.

Elias nods.

His body responds before his thoughts do—not with tension, not with anticipation, just readiness.

He realises, with a flicker of surprise, that the readiness feels different from before.

It feels unguarded.

He sets out midmorning, when the settlement has found its rhythm. The lanes are busier now. People move with purpose.

Voices overlap. The centre is not mentioned. It rarely is during daylight.

Elias walks the inner route and feels the same quiet steadiness as the day before. The markers rise ahead of him, familiar and unremarkable.

He stops where he always stops.

Nothing inside him tightens.

The lack of reaction feels almost inappropriate, like forgetting a word you've used every day of your life.

He works along the channel, checking joints and clearing small debris. The water moves freely. His notes are brief.

At one point, he becomes aware of someone standing nearby.

Maren.

She does not interrupt him. She watches for a moment, hands folded loosely, her posture attentive without being directive.

"You look well," she says finally.

Elias glances up, surprised. "Do I?"

Maren nods once. "Rested."

The word lands gently, but it carries weight.

"I slept," Elias says.

Maren's mouth curves slightly. "That helps."

They stand in silence for a moment. The rain has left the stones darker, the air cooler. Somewhere farther out, someone calls a name.

"You didn't mention the slip," Maren says, her voice even.

Elias feels the briefest flare of caution—old habit rising—but it fades quickly.

"I didn't think it mattered," he says.

Maren studies him, not searching, not testing.

"Did it?" she asks.

Elias considers the question carefully.

"I don't know yet," he says.

Maren accepts this without comment. She shifts her weight, as if deciding something.

"Sometimes," she says, "things happen that don't need to be accounted for right away."

Elias looks at her, surprised.

Maren meets his gaze calmly.

"We're allowed to let them settle," she adds.

Elias nods. Something in his chest loosens further.

Maren steps back, giving him space again in the direction of his work, then turns and leaves without instruction.

Elias watches her go, feeling a quiet gratitude he does not fully understand.

The rest of the route passes without incident. No slips. No questions. No watchers.

And yet, as Elias moves through the lanes, people respond to him slightly differently.

Not with suspicion.

With ease.

A woman speaks to him longer than necessary, finishing a story that might have ended earlier. A man laughs more freely when Elias joins him at the well. A child sits beside him on a low wall and says nothing at all.

Elias does not do anything to invite this.

He simply remains.

The effect unsettles him more than distance ever did.

That evening, as the light softens and the settlement begins to draw inward, Elias finds himself near the centre again—not crossing, not approaching, just standing where the inner lanes curve away.

He realises he is not thinking about what might happen if he went closer.

He is thinking about what has already happened.

The absence of consequence has begun to feel significant.

He turns and walks home.

Inside, the house feels larger than before. Not emptier—just less crowded with unspoken instructions. Elias sits at the small table and opens his notebook, intending to write.

He stares at the page for a long time.

Then he closes it again.

The experience resists language. Any attempt to name it feels like placing a fence where none existed.

Later, as night settles fully and the lamps glow along the lanes, Elias hears footsteps outside his window. Lio's voice drifts up, talking to someone older, his words animated.

"…he just stood there," the boy is saying. "Like it was nothing."

Elias does not know if Lio is speaking about him.

He suspects children often speak about many things at once.

Elias lies down and listens to the sounds of the settlement easing into sleep. The centre remains unseen, unremarked upon, unchanged.

For the first time, Elias understands that *after* does not mean *over*.

It means the world continues—but slightly unburdened.

What follows is not explanation.

It is adjustment.

And in the quiet recalibration of his own body—his breath, his pace, his attention—Elias senses that whatever he touched near the centre is not finished with him.

Not because it wants something.

But because it has removed something he no longer needs to carry.

The thought settles without demand.

Sleep comes.

Tomorrow will arrive.

And whatever happens next will not need to announce itself either.

Chapter 9 — Rest

Elias does not tell anyone that he is resting.

He would not know how.

The word itself feels inaccurate, too deliberate for what is happening. Rest suggests intention—something chosen, scheduled, earned. What he is experiencing arrives without effort, the way light enters a room when a curtain is moved aside.

He notices it most clearly when things go wrong.

A wheel slips from a cart near the fourth ring late in the morning, sending grain scattering across the stones. A small crowd gathers instinctively, voices rising with concern. Someone swears. Someone else begins issuing instructions too quickly.

Elias steps forward without thinking.

He does not hurry.

He kneels, rights the wheel, checks the axle, gestures for the cart to be lifted slightly. The movements are simple, unforced. People respond without question, handing him what he needs, stepping where he points.

Within minutes the grain is gathered, the cart steadied, the moment resolved.

As Elias stands, he realises something quietly startling.

His heart is not racing.

It should be. Situations like this used to tighten something in him— an urgency to fix, to prove competence, to prevent escalation. Now there is only attention. Clear, present, sufficient.

A woman thanks him, relief evident in her voice.

Elias nods and steps back.

No one applauds. No one comments on how quickly it was handled.

The settlement absorbs the incident and moves on.

Later, Bren catches up with him near the sheds.

"You handled that well," he says.

Elias shrugs. "It wasn't complicated."

Bren studies him briefly, as if hearing something unfamiliar beneath the words.

"Still," he says, then lets it drop.

Elias continues on his route, aware of the subtle shift he leaves behind him—not as admiration, but as calm.

The afternoon passes with similar moments.

A door sticks. A child trips. A disagreement flares briefly near the market stalls and then subsides.

Elias moves through it all without urgency, without the internal commentary that used to accompany every decision. He is not detached. He is present.

The difference matters.

He realises, sometime near midday, that he has stopped rehearsing conversations before they happen.

The habit had been so constant he had never named it: the quiet preparation for misunderstanding, the anticipation of correction, the bracing for disagreement. Now the space where those rehearsals lived feels open, unused.

The absence leaves room.

He sits by the well to eat, legs stretched out, back against the cool stone. The water reflects the sky in broken pieces. People come and go, drawing water, exchanging news. Elias listens without scanning for cues, without adjusting himself to fit expectations.

Lio appears again, dropping down beside him with the easy confidence of someone who has never learned to hesitate.

"You're quiet," the boy says.

Elias smiles. "I always was."

Lio shakes his head. "Not like this."

Elias considers the difference.

"I think," he says slowly, "I'm not trying as hard."

Lio grins. "Good."

Elias laughs then—an actual laugh, brief and surprised. The sound feels unfamiliar in his chest, as if it has been stored away for a long time.

The boy watches him with interest.

"You didn't get in trouble," Lio says.

"No," Elias replies.

Lio nods, satisfied. "I didn't think you would."

They sit together in silence after that, the well water moving steadily below them.

As the day wears on, Elias begins to notice how others respond to his rest.

Not everyone welcomes it.

A man speaks sharply to him when a task is delayed, irritation flaring where patience used to sit. Elias listens without defending himself, without absorbing the tone as accusation. The man's anger burns out quickly, leaving behind embarrassment.

A woman asks Elias to double-check a repair he has already completed, her voice edged with anxiety. Elias agrees without resentment and confirms what he already knows. She relaxes, grateful but unsettled.

Rest, Elias realises, does not always feel safe to those who depend on effort to hold the world together.

That evening, the elders pass him in the lane. Silas inclines his head in greeting, eyes attentive.

"You seem lighter," Silas says.

The comment is observational, not evaluative.

"I feel... less occupied," Elias replies.

Silas smiles faintly. "That can happen when we stop carrying questions that were never ours to answer."

Elias senses the interpretation being offered—the neat framing, the gentle reabsorption of change into familiar language.

He does not take it.

"Or," Elias says, "when the question changes."

Silas studies him for a moment longer, then nods.

"Perhaps," he says.

They part without tension.

At home, as the light fades, Elias sits by the window again. The centre lies beyond sight, unlit, unremarked upon. The markers do their quiet work of shaping movement, shaping habit.

Elias feels no urge to cross them.

He feels no need to prove anything to them either.

Rest has not made him passive.

It has made him accurate.

That night, as he lies down, he becomes aware of something else: the rest is not receding. It has not been spent by the day's demands. It remains, steady beneath his thoughts, like ground that does not shift when weight is placed upon it.

He understands then—not as doctrine, not as conclusion, but as simple recognition—that rest is not the absence of work.

It is the absence of fear.

The thought does not echo.

It settles.

And in that settling, Elias sleeps—deeply, evenly, without bracing for the morning to ask something of him that he cannot give.

Chapter 10 — Misunderstandings

Elias begins to look for language.

Not because he wants to explain himself to anyone, but because explanation has always been how he oriented himself in the world. Things happened, and then you named them. You placed them inside a framework sturdy enough to hold them, and life continued.

This experience refuses to stay put.

The first misunderstanding arrives quietly, dressed as concern.

It happens midmorning, when Elias is repairing a loose hinge near the grain store. A man he has worked alongside for years pauses longer than usual, watching him from the edge of the path.

"You alright?" the man asks.

Elias looks up. "Yes."

The man nods, but does not leave.

"You've seemed… different," he says finally.

Elias waits.

"Calmer," the man adds. "Not rushed."

Elias almost smiles. Almost.

"I suppose," he says.

The man shifts his weight. "After everything near the centre lately, I just wondered if—"

"If what?" Elias asks gently.

The man hesitates, then shakes his head. "Nothing. Probably just the weather."

He walks away, leaving the sentence unfinished.

Elias returns to the hinge, feeling the weight of what was not said.

Later, Silas approaches him near the records room.

"I've been thinking about our conversation," Silas says, falling into step beside him. "About unpredictability."

Elias nods.

"There are times," Silas continues, "when proximity can create a false sense of clarity. People mistake relief for understanding."

Elias hears the offer embedded in the words: a way to make sense of what is happening without letting it reshape anything too deeply.

"Possibly," Elias says.

Silas glances at him. "You don't sound convinced."

"I'm not unconvinced," Elias replies. "I'm just not sure clarity is what's happening."

Silas slows, then stops. Elias stops with him.

"What do you think it is?" Silas asks.

Elias considers the question longer than etiquette requires.

"I think," he says, "that something has stopped asking something of me."

Silas studies him with interest.

"And you believe that's… good?"

"I don't know if it's good," Elias says. "I only know it's real."

Silas nods slowly, as though filing the response away for later.

"There are experiences," he says carefully, "that feel real but still require interpretation."

Elias does not disagree.

"There are," he says. "And there are interpretations that create experiences."

Silas's smile tightens just slightly.

They part without resolution.

By afternoon, Elias notices how often people offer him explanations without waiting to hear his own.

"You've earned a break," someone says, as if rest must be justified.

"You're finally letting go," another offers, meaning surrender.

"It's good not to worry so much," a third says, framing his calm as resignation rather than presence.

Each explanation slides toward him like a stone placed carefully in a channel.

Each one would redirect the flow just enough to make the change manageable.

Elias does not take them.

Not because he wants to resist, but because none of them fit.

That evening, Maren stops him near the inner lane.

She does not speak at first. She stands with him, watching the light fade across the stones.

"People are talking," she says at last.

"About me?" Elias asks.

"About what happens when people change," Maren replies. "You happen to be nearby."

Elias absorbs this.

"They're worried," she adds.

"Of what?" he asks.

Maren exhales. "That you've found something without the proper path."

Elias nods slowly.

"And what do you think?" he asks.

Maren's gaze remains on the lane ahead.

"I think," she says, "that people trust paths more than destinations."

Elias feels the truth of it settle.

"I don't feel like I've gone anywhere," he says.

Maren turns to him then. "That," she says gently, "may be the hardest thing to accept."

As darkness settles, Elias walks home alone.

He replays the conversations of the day—not anxiously, not in self-defense, but attentively. Each misunderstanding shares a common shape: an attempt to place his experience somewhere safe, somewhere explainable, somewhere that does not require the story to change.

Elias understands why.

Stories keep people oriented.

They also keep people distant.

At home, he opens his notebook again.

This time he writes one sentence, then stops.

Nothing is wrong.

He stares at the words for a long time.

They feel incomplete. Too small. And yet they are the only ones that do not distort what he is experiencing.

He closes the notebook and sets it aside.

Some truths, he realises, cannot be clarified without being diminished.

That night, as he lies awake listening to the settlement settle around him, Elias lets go of the need to explain himself—if only for a moment.

The relief that follows is immediate.

Tomorrow, he knows, the misunderstandings will continue.

But something in him no longer feels obligated to correct them.

And in that quiet refusal, the change deepens—not outwardly, not dramatically, but inwardly, where it cannot be managed or reframed so easily.

Whatever is happening does not need consensus.

It does not even need understanding.

It only needs room.

Chapter 11 — The Interpreter

Silas chooses the moment carefully.

Not out of calculation, but out of habit. He has always believed timing is a form of respect—that words land best when the ground beneath them is stable. He approaches Elias late in the afternoon, when the work of the day has slowed and people are drifting inward, attention already loosening its grip.

They walk together without speaking at first.

The inner lanes are quiet, the stones drying after another brief shower. The markers stand ahead, unchanged, their pale lines catching the light.

Silas breaks the silence gently.

"You know," he says, "when people struggle to name something, they often reach for extremes."

Elias nods, waiting.

"They either dismiss it," Silas continues, "or they inflate it. Both are ways of protecting themselves."

"From what?" Elias asks.

Silas smiles. "From uncertainty."

They walk a few steps more.

"I've been thinking about what you said," Silas says. "About something stopping its demand on you."

Elias glances at him. "Yes?"

"It's an interesting way to frame relief," Silas says. "But it risks misunderstanding the source of that relief."

Elias slows. Silas slows with him.

"How so?" Elias asks.

Silas gestures lightly toward the centre. "Proximity can create a sense of peace. That's well documented. Familiarity lowers resistance. The body relaxes before the mind has time to assess."

Elias listens, recognising the elegance of the explanation. It is coherent. Reassuring. Useful.

"So what you're feeling," Silas continues, "may simply be a physiological response. A recalibration. Temporary."

Elias considers this.

"And if it's not?" he asks.

Silas meets his gaze calmly. "Then it will need interpretation."

They stop walking.

The lane is empty. The air feels open, unpressured.

"Interpretation by whom?" Elias asks.

Silas's answer is immediate. "By those trained to hold these things carefully."

Elias nods slowly.

"You mean the elders," he says.

"I mean people who understand the stories," Silas replies. "Who know how easily experience can mislead."

Elias feels no anger. Only clarity.

"And what if the stories are the thing that misleads?" he asks.

Silas does not react outwardly, but something in his posture tightens.

"That's a dangerous assumption," Silas says quietly. "Stories are what keep experiences from becoming chaotic."

"Or from becoming honest," Elias replies.

Silas exhales. "Honesty without framework is how people get hurt."

Elias looks toward the markers.

"I didn't get hurt," he says.

Silas follows his gaze. "Not everyone will be as… steady as you."

The words sound like a compliment. They land like a warning.

"Is that why the stories changed?" Elias asks. "To protect people from themselves?"

Silas pauses.

"To protect people from misunderstanding," he says. "And misunderstanding leads to harm."

Elias waits.

Silas continues, choosing his words with care. "You've always been responsible. That's why this concerns me. Others look to you. They will assume what you are doing is safe."

"I'm not doing anything," Elias says.

Silas smiles faintly. "Exactly."

The smile does not reach his eyes.

"Doing nothing can still teach," Silas says. "Silence can still persuade."

Elias absorbs this.

"So what would you have me do?" he asks.

Silas considers him for a long moment.

"I would have you name what you're experiencing," he says. "Publicly. Carefully. In language that keeps everyone oriented."

Elias shakes his head. "I can't."

"Why not?" Silas asks.

"Because any language I use will shrink it," Elias says. "And I don't want to lie."

Silas's expression softens, but his voice remains firm.

"Truth always requires translation," he says. "Untranslated truth is dangerous."

Elias meets his gaze steadily.

"Or," he says, "it's simply uncontrollable."

The word hangs between them.

Silas steps back slightly, creating space. Not retreating. Repositioning.

"I'm asking you to trust us," Silas says. "To trust the process that's kept this community whole."

Elias nods.

"I do trust you," he says. "I just don't trust the story you're asking me to tell."

Silas looks at him with something like sadness.

"Then you leave us very little room," he says.

Elias feels the truth of that, and it does not frighten him.

"I'm not trying to take room," he says. "I'm just not giving up the one I've been given."

Silas turns away first.

"We'll need to talk again," he says.

"Whenever you like," Elias replies.

Silas walks back toward the inner ring, his pace measured, his posture composed.

Elias remains where he is.

He notices then how differently the lane feels—not charged, not sacred, not forbidden.

Just open.

He understands something with quiet certainty:

Silas is not afraid of the centre.

Silas is afraid of what happens when it cannot be explained.

As evening settles, Elias turns and walks home.

The settlement hums around him, steady and intact.

Nothing has fractured.

Nothing has collapsed.

And yet a line has been crossed—not by Elias's feet, but by his refusal to translate what no longer needs management.

The interpreter has spoken.

And Elias, for the first time, has declined to be interpreted.

Chapter 12 — Proximity

The first time Elias notices it, he assumes it is coincidence.

He is standing near the well in the late morning, waiting his turn, when a woman he barely knows steps up beside him. She looks tired in the ordinary way—nothing dramatic, just the kind of fatigue that settles into people who manage many small things at once.

They exchange a nod.

Neither speaks.

After a moment, the woman exhales slowly, as if she has reached the end of a thought she has been holding all morning. She shifts the basket on her arm and straightens.

"Thank you," she says suddenly.

Elias turns, surprised. "For what?"

She blinks, as if realising she has spoken aloud without deciding to.

"I don't know," she admits. "I just… feel better."

A faint colour rises in her cheeks. She gives a small, apologetic smile and steps forward when the well clears, conversation complete.

Elias watches her go, unsettled.

It happens again that afternoon.

He is repairing a cracked stone near the market path when a man stops nearby, waiting rather than passing around him as people usually do. The man does not speak. He simply stands there, hands resting loosely at his sides.

After a minute, the man clears his throat.

"I always rush this part of the day," he says, as if continuing a conversation they have already begun. "I don't know why."

Elias looks up. "Do you need to get through?"

The man shakes his head. "No. I just... realised I don't have to."

They stand together for a moment longer. Then the man nods once and walks on, unhurried.

Elias finishes the repair with a faint unease growing in his chest.

He has not done anything.

He has not spoken differently. He has not offered comfort or advice. He has not tried to create calm.

And yet calm seems to be occurring.

By evening, he has begun to notice a pattern.

People linger near him. Conversations stretch longer than necessary. Silence becomes less awkward, more inhabitable.

Children sit beside him without being asked. Adults pause mid-task, then resume more slowly, as if remembering something they had misplaced.

Elias does not feel powerful.

He feels exposed.

He remembers Silas's words: *Silence can still persuade.*

The thought troubles him.

He does not want to influence anyone. He does not want to become a reference point, a quiet authority others begin orienting themselves around.

He does not want proximity to become expectation.

That night, he chooses a longer route home, deliberately passing through the outer ring where movement is brisk and purpose-driven. He hopes the change in pace will settle whatever is happening.

It does not.

At a narrow crossing, he pauses to let a small group pass. One of them—a woman with lines of constant worry etched into her face—meets his eyes and hesitates.

"You're Elias, aren't you?" she asks.

"Yes," he says.

She nods slowly. "I thought so."

She does not explain how she knows his name.

"I don't usually stop," she says, gesturing vaguely toward the inner lanes. "I don't like the way it makes me feel."

"And now?" Elias asks.

She considers the question carefully.

"Now it feels quieter," she says. "Not safe. Just… quieter."

The distinction matters.

She thanks him again, unnecessarily, and moves on.

Elias reaches his house with a weight settling into him—not fear, but responsibility he has not asked for.

He eats alone, distracted, replaying the day. Each interaction seems small on its own. Together they form something that feels dangerously like momentum.

Later, as darkness gathers, he walks toward the inner lanes again, not to approach the centre, but to test himself. To see whether the sense of influence diminishes with distance.

Near the markers, he stops.

The air is cool. The stones are dry. The square lies beyond, pale and quiet.

Two people stand nearby, speaking in low voices. When Elias arrives, they fall silent—not abruptly, not with alarm, but with attention. One of them smiles.

"We were just talking," the man says, "about how tense everyone's been lately."

The woman beside him nods. "And how strange it is when that eases."

They look at Elias as if he is part of the answer.

"I'm not doing anything," Elias says, the words leaving him before he can soften them.

The man lifts his hands slightly. "We know. That's what's odd."

Elias feels a flicker of frustration rise—his first in days.

"I don't want this," he says.

The woman tilts her head. "What?"

"To be something people come near because they feel better," Elias replies. "I don't want to replace one kind of dependence with another."

The man studies him with new respect.

"Then don't," he says simply.

Elias exhales.

"Closeness doesn't have to mean control," the woman adds. "We know that."

Elias is not sure they do.

He stands there a moment longer, then turns away, walking back toward the third ring.

Behind him, the centre remains where it always has—unchanged, unresponsive to the subtle currents now moving around it.

Elias understands something then, with a clarity that does not feel like insight but like recognition:

What people are responding to is not him.

It is the absence of fear in him.

Fear has been such a constant presence that its absence registers like warmth on skin long kept cold.

Proximity does not create this.

It reveals it.

The real danger, Elias realises, is not that others are being drawn to him.

It is that those responsible for managing fear will notice it spreading without permission.

That night, sleep comes more lightly.

Not because Elias is anxious.

But because something has shifted from personal to communal.

The rest he has discovered is no longer contained within his own body.

It is beginning to move.

And once movement begins, stories have a way of tightening their grip.

Chapter 13 — Concern

The elders do not call it a meeting at first.

They gather in the way people gather when they do not want to admit they are gathering—one arriving early to straighten papers that do not need straightening, another lingering after a routine conversation, a third stepping in as if passing through and then staying.

The records room is dim in the late afternoon, the air cool and still. Rain taps softly at the small window, not demanding entry, just present.

Silas is already seated when Maren arrives. He has a book open in front of him, though his eyes are not on the page. Two other elders sit nearby—quiet, attentive, neither eager nor reluctant. They have the posture of people who know that something is being held.

Maren sets her hands on the edge of the table.

"This isn't discipline," she says immediately.

Silas looks up. "No one is suggesting discipline."

Maren holds his gaze. "Good."

Silas's mouth tightens slightly, then relaxes. He closes the book gently, as if to signal he is fully present now.

"People are unsettled," he says.

"They're always unsettled," one of the other elders replies. A younger man, earnest, with a tendency toward certainty. "The weather unsettles them. The market unsettles them. A child's fever unsettles them."

Silas nods. "This is different."

Maren does not speak yet. She listens.

The third elder—a woman older than Maren, quieter, with eyes that seem to hold more history than her face reveals—leans forward.

"It's spreading," she says softly.

The word lands heavier than it should have, as if it carries something contagious.

Silas gestures lightly, acknowledging. "People have begun to associate Elias with… relief."

The younger elder frowns. "That's not a problem."

"It can become one," Silas replies.

Maren's hands remain steady on the table. "Why?"

Silas looks at her as if the answer is obvious.

"Because relief without framework makes people careless," he says. "They stop listening. They stop distinguishing. They stop honouring process."

"Or they stop being afraid," the younger elder says.

Silas turns his gaze toward him, calm but firm. "Fear is not the point."

The younger elder hesitates. "Isn't it?"

Silas's eyes sharpen slightly. "Care is the point."

Maren speaks then, her voice quiet but clear.

"And care is not the same as fear," she says.

Silas exhales through his nose, a sound that might have been patience.

"I agree," he says. "In theory."

Maren's expression does not change.

Silas continues, choosing words carefully. "But in practice, fear has been the mechanism that ensures care is obeyed. Remove fear too quickly and you remove compliance."

The room goes still.

One of the elders shifts, uncomfortable.

Maren's gaze stays on Silas. "That's a revealing way to say it," she replies.

Silas does not flinch. "It's an honest way."

Maren's voice remains gentle. "Honesty without wisdom is still dangerous."

Silas's mouth twitches faintly at the reversal of his own phrase, but he lets it pass.

"We need to decide what we're doing," the older woman says softly, interrupting before the room becomes a debate. "Because the settlement is already deciding without us."

Silas nods once. "Exactly."

Maren draws in a slow breath.

"What do you propose?" she asks.

Silas's fingers rest on the closed book, as if grounding himself.

"I propose we speak with Elias again," he says. "Together. Not privately. Not as a confrontation. But as a clarification."

"Clarification of what?" the younger elder asks.

Silas glances toward the window, where rain blurs the world outside.

"Of the story," he says simply.

Maren's face tightens slightly. "And what story would you have him tell?"

Silas looks back at her. "One that keeps people oriented," he says. "One that reminds them that the centre is not an ordinary place, and that closeness requires readiness."

Maren hears the pressure beneath the words.

"You want him to restore the markers," she says.

Silas's expression remains calm. "I want him to prevent harm."

The younger elder leans forward. "Has there been harm?"

Silas pauses. The pause is not uncertainty. It is strategy.

"Not yet," he says.

The older woman's voice is barely above a whisper. "We've always acted before harm."

Maren's eyes lower briefly, then lift again. "Or we've always assumed harm would come."

The room holds that sentence like something fragile.

Silas speaks carefully. "Maren, you've always understood that the centre is not meant to be approached casually."

"I understand that people were taught that," Maren replies.

Silas's gaze hardens for a moment.

"This is not the time for philosophical nuance," he says.

Maren's voice does not rise. "It's always the time," she replies. "Because what we decide now will become another layer of story."

The younger elder looks between them, uncertain which kind of authority to follow.

The older woman closes her eyes briefly, as if listening to something beyond the room.

"We are responsible for the settlement," she says. "Not for Elias's experience."

Silas nods. "Yes."

Maren's hands shift slightly on the table, the first sign of strain.

"And are we responsible for the fear we've built into it?" she asks.

Silas looks at her steadily. "We are responsible for keeping people safe."

Maren's gaze does not move. "Safety is not the same as control."

Silas's voice stays even. "Control is sometimes what safety requires."

The sentence lands like a door closing.

No one speaks for a moment.

Rain continues at the window.

The older woman opens her eyes again.

"We should invite Elias to speak at the next gathering," she says, as if concluding a practical matter. "Not to confess. Not to defend himself. Simply to name what he's experiencing."

Maren's jaw tightens.

Silas nods. "That would be appropriate."

"And if he refuses?" the younger elder asks.

Silas's gaze is steady.

"Then we will have learned something," he says.

Maren looks at him sharply. "What?"

Silas does not answer immediately.

"That he is unwilling to carry the community with him," he says finally. "That he is choosing a private truth over a shared one."

Maren hears the trap in the words.

"A shared truth should not require coercion," she says.

Silas's expression softens slightly, almost regretful.

"Coercion isn't required," he says. "Only responsibility."

Maren leans back slowly, as if easing away from the table before her own body is forced into a posture she does not want to inhabit.

The older woman gathers a few papers that have not been used.

"We'll speak with him," she says. "Soon."

The elders begin to rise, the meeting dissolving back into ordinary movement. No one calls it a decision. No one names it as fear. It is framed as care, as responsibility, as wisdom.

When Maren leaves last, she pauses at the door and looks back at Silas.

"Be careful," she says quietly.

Silas lifts his eyes. "Always."

Maren's mouth tightens at the answer, then softens.

"You know what I mean," she says.

Silas holds her gaze.

"So do you," he replies.

Maren steps out into the damp evening, the door closing behind her with a soft, final sound.

Outside, the settlement continues as if nothing has happened.

People cook. Children laugh. Doors close. Lamps are lit. The rain eases into mist.

Elias walks home somewhere among them, unaware that concern has been gathered, named, and set into motion.

Not as punishment.

As protection.

And in the careful hands of those who manage stories, protection has always been the first step toward tightening.

Chapter 14 — The Loyal Ones

The first person to speak to Elias is not an elder.

That is how he knows it matters.

Jonah finds him near the outer ring, where the path widens and the settlement feels less watchful. They have known each other for years—not closely, not intimately, but with the steady familiarity that comes from shared work and mutual reliability.

Jonah is dependable. He follows rules without resenting them. He believes most systems exist for good reasons, even when those reasons are not immediately clear.

He is, Elias realises, exactly the kind of person the settlement relies on.

"You've been hard to catch," Jonah says, falling into step beside him.

"I didn't know I was hiding," Elias replies.

Jonah smiles briefly, then lets it fade. "You're not."

They walk together for a moment in silence.

"I wanted to talk to you," Jonah says. "Not officially. Just… man to man."

Elias nods. "Alright."

Jonah slows near a low wall and rests a hand on it, as if grounding himself before continuing.

"People are uneasy," he says. "You know that."

"I do," Elias replies.

"And I know you're not trying to cause trouble," Jonah continues quickly. "That's important. Everyone knows that."

Elias hears the unspoken addition: *which is why this is difficult.*

"I don't feel like I'm doing anything," Elias says.

Jonah exhales. "That's what worries them."

Elias looks at him. "Why?"

Jonah hesitates, searching for words that won't sound like accusation.

"Because influence without intention is unpredictable," he says finally. "At least when people argue, you know where they stand."

Elias absorbs this.

"So silence feels dangerous," he says.

Jonah nods. "Silence feels like permission."

They resume walking.

Jonah's voice lowers slightly, though no one is near enough to overhear.

"The elders are concerned," he says. "Not about you. About what might follow."

"Follow what?" Elias asks.

Jonah gestures vaguely inward. "This... loosening."

Elias considers the word.

"It doesn't feel like loosening to me," he says. "It feels like steadiness."

Jonah glances at him sharply. "That's exactly it."

They stop walking again.

"Steadiness makes people wonder what they've been holding themselves against," Jonah says. "And once they start wondering, they stop bracing."

Elias meets his gaze. "Is that a problem?"

Jonah looks away.

"It can be," he says. "If people stop bracing all at once."

The phrase carries more fear than Jonah realises.

Elias softens his voice. "Jonah, do you feel unsafe?"

Jonah shakes his head quickly. "No. I feel… responsible."

"For whom?" Elias asks.

Jonah's answer comes without hesitation. "For everyone."

Elias nods slowly. "That's a heavy thing to carry."

Jonah's jaw tightens. "Someone has to."

They stand in the widening space of the outer ring, the settlement stretching around them. People move past without slowing, unaware of the quiet pressure gathering beneath ordinary conversation.

"I don't want you to get hurt," Jonah says suddenly.

Elias believes him.

"Thank you," he says.

"And I don't want people getting confused," Jonah adds. "Confusion makes people reckless."

"Or honest," Elias replies gently.

Jonah laughs once, without humour. "That's easy to say when you're not the one responsible for keeping things from falling apart."

Elias feels the weight of that sentence settle.

"I'm not asking anyone to follow me," he says.

Jonah nods. "I know. But they are watching you anyway."

They walk again, slower now.

"You'll be asked to speak," Jonah says. "Soon."

Elias does not pretend surprise. "About what?"

"About what's happening," Jonah says. "So people can place it."

"And if I don't?" Elias asks.

Jonah stops.

The loyalty in his face is unmistakable—and painful.

"Then it becomes harder for me to defend you," he says quietly.

Elias understands the cost embedded in the words.

"You shouldn't have to defend me," he says.

Jonah looks at him, eyes searching.

"That's not how communities work," he says.

Elias nods. "That may be the problem."

Jonah exhales sharply, frustration rising. "Why are you doing this?"

The question is raw enough to deserve honesty.

"I'm not," Elias says. "That's what I keep trying to tell people."

Jonah stares at him, then looks away again.

"You've changed," he says.

"Yes," Elias agrees.

"Then help us understand how," Jonah says.

Elias shakes his head slowly.

"I can't explain it without turning it into something smaller," he says. "And I don't want to lie just to make people comfortable."

Jonah's shoulders sag slightly.

"You're making this very hard," he says.

"I know," Elias replies.

They stand in silence for a long moment.

Jonah straightens at last. "I hope you'll reconsider," he says. "For everyone's sake."

Elias meets his eyes. "I hope you'll notice what you're asking me to give up."

Jonah does not respond.

He turns and walks back toward the inner rings, his posture rigid with the weight of loyalty pulling in two directions.

Elias remains where he is.

He watches the settlement move, the paths curving as they always have, the centre unseen but present.

He feels no anger toward Jonah.

Only sadness.

Loyalty, he realises, is often the most painful thing to question— not because it is wrong, but because it is sincere.

That evening, as the light fades and the lanes soften, Elias understands something with clarity that does not feel like insight but like acceptance:

The next pressure will not come from authority.

It will come from love.

And love, when afraid, can ask for sacrifices fear never could.

Chapter 15 — Boundaries

The changes arrive quietly.

Not announced. Not debated. Just adjusted—small shifts in language, minor clarifications folded into routine notices, practical decisions framed as common sense.

No one calls them new rules.

They are called reminders.

Elias notices the first one on a board near the sheds, written in a familiar hand.

Inner lane work to be scheduled in pairs until further notice.

The note is brief, reasonable, impossible to argue with without sounding reckless.

He reads it twice.

Bren appears beside him, glancing at the board.

"Temporary," Bren says. "Just while things settle."

Elias nods. "Of course."

Bren hesitates, then adds, "Not because of you."

Elias meets his gaze. "I didn't think it was."

Bren seems relieved by the answer and moves on.

Later that day, Elias is reassigned from an inner route to a perimeter check without explanation. The work is fine. Necessary. But the pattern is clear enough to register.

Distance is being redistributed.

At the well, he overhears a conversation between two women he knows well enough to greet but not well enough to interrupt.

"They're just making sure everyone's safe," one says.

"It makes sense," the other replies. "Things were getting a bit... loose."

Loose.

The word catches in Elias's chest.

He continues past them without comment.

By midday, the inner lanes feel different.

Not forbidden.

Managed.

An elder lingers near the markers longer than necessary. A younger worker redirects a child with unusual firmness. People pause at the edge of the square, then turn away as if remembering something important at the last moment.

Care has become choreography.

Elias walks his assigned route and feels the pressure not as restriction, but as expectation—the subtle pull to behave in ways that confirm the new shape is necessary.

He does not resist.

Resistance would clarify the boundary too sharply.

Instead, he remains as he has been—present, unhurried, unafraid.

The contrast grows sharper.

That afternoon, Maren finds him near the third ring.

"They're tightening things," she says, not accusing, simply stating what both of them can see.

"Yes," Elias replies.

Maren studies his face. "You don't seem surprised."

"I am," Elias says. "Just not confused."

She exhales. "Silas believes clarity will calm people."

"And you?" Elias asks.

Maren's mouth tightens slightly. "I think clarity often creates the thing it's trying to prevent."

They walk together for a short distance.

"You could help," Maren says quietly.

Elias stops.

"By explaining," she continues. "By reassuring people that what you're experiencing isn't... transferable."

Elias feels the request land where Jonah's had—softly, painfully.

"It is transferable," he says.

Maren looks at him sharply. "Elias—"

"Not because of me," he adds quickly. "Because fear isn't the source of calm. Its absence is."

Maren looks away, troubled.

"They'll hear that as destabilising," she says.

"I know," Elias replies.

Maren turns back to him. "Then you see why they're setting boundaries."

"Yes," Elias says. "I just don't agree with what they're protecting."

Maren's eyes search his face. "And what do you think they're protecting?"

Elias does not answer immediately.

"The story," he says finally. "Not the people."

Maren closes her eyes briefly.

"That story kept us alive," she says.

Elias nods. "For a time."

They stand together in silence, the settlement moving around them.

Later, Elias passes the markers again.

This time, there is a rope.

Not a barrier. Not tied tight. Just looped between two posts, low enough to step over without effort.

Symbolic.

He stops and looks at it.

A man nearby clears his throat.

"They're just making it clearer," the man says, half-apologetic. "So no one misunderstands."

Elias meets his eyes.

"Clearer than what?" he asks.

The man frowns, then shrugs. "Clearer than before."

Elias nods and moves on.

That evening, notices are read aloud at the gathering.

Nothing dramatic.

Just small adjustments. New scheduling. Shared responsibility. Emphasis on readiness and process.

Words like *safety*, *care*, and *wisdom* appear frequently.

Fear is never mentioned.

Elias listens from the edge.

No one looks at him directly.

He feels the boundaries settle—not around the centre, but around conversation, behaviour, expectation.

The settlement is not closing.

It is aligning.

At home, Elias sits by the window again, watching the lanes dim under the lamps. The rope near the markers is barely visible from here, but he knows it's there.

He does not feel anger.

He feels grief.

Boundaries, he realises, are rarely built because something is dangerous.

They are built because something is uncontrollable.

And uncontrollable things expose how much control has been mistaken for care.

As night deepens, Elias understands with quiet certainty:

No one will force him to cross a line.

They will simply keep redrawing them until he no longer knows where to stand.

The thought steadies him rather than frightens him.

Because lines that move are not lines that hold truth.

They are lines that protect fear from being seen.

And fear, once named by its shape, has already begun to loosen.

Chapter 16 — Children

The children notice before the adults admit it.

They always do.

The first sign comes in the morning, when Elias passes the small square near the third ring and sees a cluster of children gathered closer to the inner lanes than they usually are. They are not running. They are not daring one another.

They are sitting.

On the low stones. On the ground. On the edges of steps that curve inward before turning away again. Their bodies are loose, unguarded, as if they have forgotten there is a reason not to be here.

An elder stands nearby, watching too closely.

When one of the children shifts forward, the elder steps in quickly.

"Careful," she says. "Not there."

The child looks up. "Why?"

The elder hesitates, then smiles. "Because it's not for play."

The child considers this, then shrugs and scoots back a few inches—obedient, but unconvinced.

Elias continues on, something tight in his chest loosening and tightening at the same time.

Later that day, he hears laughter near the inner lanes.

Lio is there, of course, balanced on a stone near the curve, arms outstretched, pretending the ground is water. Two younger children watch him, wide-eyed.

"You'll fall," one of them says.

"So?" Lio replies cheerfully. "It's just ground."

An elder approaches, concern sharpening her steps.

"Lio," she says, reaching out. "That's enough."

Lio hops down easily.

"You're too close," she adds.

Lio looks around. "Close to what?"

The elder's mouth opens, then closes again.

"To the centre," she says finally.

Lio nods. "It's been there the whole time."

The elder exhales, patience thinning. "You know what I mean."

Lio tilts his head. "I don't think I do."

Elias does not intervene.

He knows better now.

Children do not need rescuing from questions.

They need space to hold them.

By afternoon, the pattern is unmistakable.

Children linger where adults hesitate. They cross invisible lines without realising lines exist. They sit near the rope between the markers, duck under it, step over it, forget it entirely.

No harm comes to them.

What comes instead is stillness.

Adults watch from a distance, nervous in the way people are nervous when their explanations fail to land.

At the well, Elias overhears a sharp exchange.

"They're setting a bad example," someone mutters.

"They're children," another replies.

"That's exactly the problem," the first insists. "They don't know what they're doing."

Elias hears the fear beneath the words: *They aren't afraid enough.*

That evening, at the gathering, the elders address it carefully.

"We've noticed increased activity near the inner lanes," Silas says, his voice calm and steady. "Please help us guide the children with care."

Parents nod. Some glance toward the markers, then toward their children, uncertainty flickering.

A hand goes up.

It belongs to a woman Elias recognises as thoughtful, rarely reactive.

"What harm has come to them?" she asks.

Silas smiles gently. "None."

"Then what are we preventing?" she asks.

Silas's smile holds.

"Potential harm," he says.

The woman nods slowly. "Based on what?"

The room stills.

Silas answers carefully. "Based on wisdom."

Elias watches as the woman absorbs the response.

"Whose?" she asks quietly.

A murmur ripples through the gathering.

Silas's eyes flick briefly toward Maren, then back.

"Shared wisdom," he says.

The woman lowers her hand, unsatisfied but not defiant.

The gathering moves on.

Afterward, Elias finds Lio sitting near the rope again, fingers tracing patterns in the dust.

"They told us to stay back," Lio says without looking up.

"Yes," Elias replies.

"But they didn't tell us why," Lio continues.

"No," Elias agrees.

Lio looks up then, eyes searching Elias's face.

"Do you think the centre doesn't like children?" he asks.

The question is soft enough to hurt.

Elias kneels so he is level with the boy.

"I think," he says carefully, "that the centre doesn't mind children at all."

Lio smiles, relief immediate.

"Good," he says. "Because I don't think it likes being lonely."

Elias feels something break open in his chest—not pain, but recognition.

As night falls, the children drift home, guided more firmly now by parents who have been gently instructed. The inner lanes empty again.

The rope remains.

Elias walks the edge of the square once more, watching how the absence of children makes the space feel tighter, more managed.

He understands something with quiet clarity:

Children do not move toward the centre because they are brave.

They move toward it because they have not yet learned to fear what has never harmed them.

Fear must be taught.

So must distance.

As Elias turns away, he senses the pressure building—not from rebellion, not from defiance, but from innocence exposing the story's thin places.

The elders will respond.

They must.

Because nothing threatens a managed system more than children who refuse to be afraid.

And nothing reveals truth more clearly than lives that have not yet learned where they are supposed to stand.

Chapter 17 — Readiness

Maren has been awake for hours when Elias finds her.

She sits on the low bench near the western edge of the inner lanes, hands folded in her lap, watching the light shift across the stone. The settlement has not fully woken yet. The hour belongs to those who carry things quietly.

She does not look surprised to see him.

"You walk early now," she says.

Elias stops a few paces away. "So do you."

Maren nods. "Some habits are hard to unlearn."

They sit together without speaking for a moment. The air is cool. The rope near the markers hangs slack, unmoving.

"I wanted to talk," Elias says finally.

"I know," Maren replies.

He studies her face, noticing the lines there not as age but as accumulation—decisions made, pressures absorbed, questions postponed until they hardened into responsibilities.

"They're using the word *readiness* a lot," Elias says.

Maren exhales slowly. "Yes."

"What does it mean?" he asks.

Maren's gaze stays on the lane ahead. "It means people want assurance before they release control."

Elias nods. "And who decides when someone is ready?"

Maren's mouth tightens slightly. "Those who fear what happens if they're wrong."

The honesty costs her something. Elias can feel it.

"They've always said readiness was about wisdom," he says.

"And sometimes it is," Maren replies. "But sometimes it's about delay."

She turns to him then, eyes steady.

"Elias," she says, "do you know why I've stayed as long as I have?"

He shakes his head.

"Because I believed that if I stayed, I could soften things," she says. "Slow the tightening. Translate care away from fear."

"And did it work?" Elias asks.

Maren's lips curve in something like a smile. "Sometimes."

She looks back toward the markers.

"But I'm tired," she continues. "Tired of explaining why gentleness matters. Tired of defending space. Tired of watching fear dress itself up as responsibility and call that faithfulness."

The word *tired* lands heavily. It carries more truth than complaint.

"They're asking me to support the gathering," Maren says. "To stand with them when they invite you to speak."

Elias feels the weight of it.

"And will you?" he asks.

Maren is quiet for a long moment.

"I don't know," she says. "If I stand with them, I help contain what's happening. If I don't, I become part of the problem they're trying to manage."

Elias does not rush her.

"I don't want to fracture the settlement," she says softly. "I've spent my life protecting it."

"I know," Elias replies.

"And yet," she adds, "something in me knows that what you're carrying isn't dangerous."

Elias feels a quiet gratitude rise—not relief, but recognition.

"They're afraid you'll lead people where they're not ready to go," Maren says.

"I'm not leading anyone," Elias says.

"I know," Maren replies. "That's what frightens them."

She turns fully toward him now.

"Readiness," she says, "has always been framed as something you achieve. As if people become ready by accumulating enough instruction, enough caution, enough fear."

Elias listens.

"But I'm beginning to think," Maren continues, "that readiness might be something you discover when fear loosens its grip."

Elias feels the truth of it settle.

"They'll say that's irresponsible," he says.

"They already are," Maren replies.

They sit in silence again, the settlement slowly stirring around them.

"I need to ask you something," Maren says.

Elias turns to her.

"If they ask you to speak," she says, "will you?"

He considers the question carefully.

"I'll stand there," he says. "I'll answer honestly if someone asks me something directly. But I won't frame this in a way that manages people's fear."

Maren nods. "They'll hear that as refusal."

"Then it is," Elias says.

Maren closes her eyes briefly.

"And if they restrict you further?" she asks. "If they ask you to step back? To remove yourself from places where people feel... influenced?"

Elias thinks of Jonah. Of loyalty. Of the cost that follows love when fear enters it.

"I'll stay," he says. "I won't hide. I won't provoke. I won't leave."

Maren opens her eyes.

"That's harder than rebellion," she says.

"I know," Elias replies.

She studies him, something like admiration and sorrow mingling in her gaze.

"You're not trying to win," she says.

112

"No," Elias agrees. "I'm trying to remain."

Maren lets out a slow breath, as if something in her has finally been allowed to rest.

"That may be the most threatening posture of all," she says.

They rise together as the light strengthens.

Before leaving, Maren reaches out and touches Elias's arm—not as authority, not as reassurance, but as acknowledgement.

"Whatever happens," she says, "don't let them convince you that readiness is something you owe."

Elias meets her gaze.

"I won't," he says.

Maren turns and walks back toward the inner ring, shoulders squared, carrying both loyalty and truth with visible effort.

Elias remains for a moment longer, looking toward the markers.

Readiness, he realises, has never been about approaching the centre.

It has been about trusting that nothing essential needs to be defended.

He turns and walks home, steady, unhurried.

The gathering will come.

The pressure will increase.

But something in him is already settled.

Whatever readiness truly is, it has arrived—not as permission, not as achievement, but as the quiet absence of fear.

And that, he knows, will not be easily contained.

Chapter 18 — Staying

Elias does not leave.

This is the first thing people notice.

Not because anyone expected him to disappear, but because disappearance would have made sense. It would have been tidy. Interpretable. Leaving is a familiar response when pressure increases—proof that something has gone wrong, reassurance that order will restore itself.

Staying confuses the story.

The days following the conversation with Maren feel narrower, as if the settlement has drawn its breath and is holding it. Elias feels it in small ways: conversations that end sooner than they used to, glances that linger just long enough to register uncertainty, work assignments adjusted without explanation.

He is not excluded.

He is accommodated.

The distinction matters.

Elias continues his routines. He walks the lanes. He repairs what needs repairing. He eats where he always has. He stands where he always has.

He does not cross new lines.

He does not announce himself.

He simply remains.

At first, people test this.

A woman pauses mid-sentence when he approaches, watching to see if he will fill the silence with reassurance or retreat from it. He does neither. She resumes speaking on her own, voice steadier than before.

A man makes a pointed comment about "respecting process," eyes flicking toward Elias as if waiting for reaction. Elias nods politely and keeps walking. The comment dissolves without conflict.

Someone else thanks him too earnestly for something ordinary, then looks embarrassed, as if realising gratitude has been misplaced.

Elias absorbs it all without adjusting his posture.

Staying, he realises, is not passive.

It requires more attention than leaving ever would.

One afternoon, Jonah approaches him again.

This time his tone is gentler, less burdened by responsibility.

"You could make this easier," Jonah says.

Elias waits.

"You could take a few days away from the inner lanes," Jonah continues. "Let things cool down."

"And then?" Elias asks.

Jonah hesitates. "Then people would relax."

Elias nods slowly. "About what?"

Jonah looks away. "About you."

Elias feels the familiar ache of loyalty tug again.

"If I leave," Elias says, "what does that teach them?"

Jonah exhales. "That you're willing to compromise."

"Or that fear sets the terms," Elias replies.

Jonah does not answer.

They part without resolution, the space between them carrying more weight than words.

That evening, Elias walks near the centre again, not closer than he is allowed, not farther away than he needs to be. The rope remains slack. The markers stand unchanged.

Two elders pass nearby, voices low. Elias catches fragments.

"…still unsettled…"
"…best not to rush…"
"…he's not helping…"

He does not stop to listen.

Staying is not about monitoring reaction.

It is about refusing to be shaped by it.

At home, Elias sits at the table and opens his notebook.

He writes:

Staying is not agreement.

He pauses, then adds another line.

It is presence without permission.

He closes the notebook.

The words feel right, but incomplete.

Later, he is invited—politely, carefully—to attend a smaller gathering, one not officially announced. The invitation is framed as inclusion, not summons.

He attends.

The conversation circles familiar ground. Safety. Wisdom. Community. Responsibility. Elias listens more than he speaks. When asked directly, he answers simply, without qualification.

"I'm not asking anyone to change," he says at one point. "I'm not offering an alternative system. I'm just not afraid of what I've encountered."

The room grows quiet.

Someone clears their throat.

"That may be enough to change things," another says.

Elias meets their gaze.

"Only if fear was what held them together," he replies.

No one argues.

Afterward, Maren finds him at the edge of the lane.

"They're frustrated," she says.

"I know," Elias replies.

"They don't know how to move you," she adds.

Elias smiles faintly. "I'm not trying to be moved."

Maren studies him with something like relief.

"You're not trying to win," she says again.

"No," Elias agrees. "I'm trying to stay where I am."

As night falls, Elias walks home under the lamps, their light soft and steady. The settlement holds its shape, but the effort is showing now—the careful maintenance, the constant reassurance.

Elias feels no triumph.

Only patience.

Staying, he understands, is not about endurance.

It is about trust.

Trust that what is real does not require retreat to survive pressure.

Trust that truth does not need urgency.

Trust that presence, when unafraid, eventually reveals what fear has been hiding.

He lies down that night and sleeps without bracing.

Tomorrow, the gathering will come.

Questions will be asked.

Stories will tighten or loosen.

Elias will not decide the outcome.

He will only stay.

And in that staying, something irreversible has already occurred:

Fear has lost the power to move him.

And that, more than any argument, has begun to change everything.

Chapter 19 — The Question of Authority

They meet him at the edge of the square.

Not at the centre. Not in the records room. Not in a private space where words could be shaped without witnesses. This location is deliberate—public enough to be seen, restrained enough to feel orderly.

Authority prefers thresholds.

Elias arrives alone. He has not been summoned with urgency, only invited—carefully, respectfully—to "talk." The phrase carries weight without admitting it does.

Silas stands with two other elders. Maren is there as well, a step to the side rather than at the centre of the group. Her posture is calm, but Elias can see the strain in her shoulders.

People linger at a distance, pretending not to watch.

Silas speaks first.

"Thank you for coming," he says.

Elias nods. "Of course."

Silas gestures toward the stone bench near the markers. They sit. The rope hangs loose behind them, a line without force.

"We want to speak plainly," Silas says.

Elias waits.

"There's concern," Silas continues. "About influence."

Elias hears the word land exactly where it is meant to.

"Influence isn't something I'm claiming," he replies.

"Nevertheless," Silas says, "it's something you're exerting."

Elias considers the framing.

"People are responding to me," he says. "That's different."

Silas leans forward slightly. "Response creates direction."

"Only if it's managed," Elias replies.

One of the other elders—a man with a practical manner—interjects.

"This isn't about blame," he says. "It's about responsibility. Authority exists to protect the community."

Elias nods. "I agree."

The elder relaxes slightly, relieved by the agreement.

"And authority," Elias adds, "is not the same as control."

The relief fades.

Silas's gaze sharpens, but his voice remains composed.

"Authority must sometimes limit freedom," he says. "Especially when freedom becomes destabilising."

Elias looks past them, toward the square.

"Who decides when freedom is destabilising?" he asks.

Silas answers without hesitation. "Those entrusted with care."

"And how do you recognise that trust?" Elias asks.

Silas pauses.

"By role," he says. "By history. By consensus."

Elias nods slowly.

"And if authority must be enforced to remain credible?" he asks.

Silas's mouth tightens.

"Authority doesn't require enforcement," he says. "It requires cooperation."

"Which you achieve how?" Elias asks gently.

Silence stretches.

Maren speaks then, her voice quiet but steady.

"By fear," she says.

The word lands heavily.

Silas turns toward her. "Maren—"

She does not back down. "We've already said it," she continues. "We just prefer not to hear it out loud."

The practical elder shifts uncomfortably.

"We teach caution," he says.

"We teach fear," Maren replies. "And we call it care."

Silas exhales. "This isn't helpful."

"It's honest," Elias says.

Silas turns back to him. "Elias, no one is questioning your sincerity."

"I know," Elias replies.

"What we're questioning," Silas continues, "is whether your posture undermines the authority that keeps this place intact."

Elias meets his gaze.

"Does authority that depends on fear deserve to remain intact?" he asks.

The question is not defiant.

It is sincere.

Silas's voice cools slightly.

"You're framing this as a philosophical issue," he says. "It's not. It's practical."

"Then let's be practical," Elias says. "What are you asking me to do?"

Silas gestures subtly toward the markers.

"We're asking you to step back," he says. "To reduce proximity. To allow people space to reorient."

Elias absorbs the request.

"For how long?" he asks.

Silas hesitates. "Until things stabilise."

"And who decides when that is?" Elias asks.

Silas meets his gaze. "We do."

Elias nods.

"I won't," he says.

The refusal is quiet.

Final.

Silas stiffens. "You're leaving us no choice."

"No," Elias replies. "I'm leaving you with a choice you don't like."

The practical elder speaks quickly. "We're not threatening you."

"I know," Elias says. "You're protecting your authority."

Silas's voice sharpens. "We're protecting people."

Elias stands slowly.

"So am I," he says. "By refusing to pretend fear is love."

A murmur ripples through the onlookers.

Silas rises as well.

"You are not above this community," he says.

"I'm not trying to be," Elias replies. "I'm just not beneath it."

The distinction unsettles something deep.

Maren stands too, stepping closer to Elias without touching him.

"This is the moment," she says quietly to Silas. "Where you decide whether authority serves life—or demands it."

Silas looks at her, then at Elias.

"We'll continue this," he says.

"I'm here," Elias replies.

Silas turns away first, the elders following.

The gathering disperses, tension settling into the stones like a held breath.

Elias remains by the markers.

No punishment has been issued.

No boundary enforced.

And yet the question has been asked aloud now, where it cannot be unheard:

Is authority something that protects truth—

Or something that must be protected from it?

Elias turns and walks home, unhurried.

The settlement holds, but the strain is visible now, like a structure asked to bear weight it was never meant to carry.

And somewhere beneath it all, unchanged and untroubled, the centre remains—

Unimpressed by authority.

Unmoved by fear.

Still there.

Chapter 20 — Without Leverage

No consequences follow.

Not immediately.

This, more than anything else, unsettles the settlement.

Elias is not removed from his work. No public statement is issued. No new boundary is announced to explain what has just occurred. Life continues with the same careful rhythm it always has, as if waiting to see what will happen if nothing happens.

Authority hesitates when leverage fails.

Elias feels the shift in subtler ways.

Assignments arrive later than usual. Requests are framed more carefully. Conversations feel tentative, as if people are testing the edges of something newly fragile.

He continues his days as before.

He does not explain himself.

He does not gather supporters.

He does not seek vindication.

He does not retreat.

Without leverage, there is nothing for him to push against—and nothing for authority to push with.

The effect is disorienting.

People approach him now with different questions.

Not "What do you believe?"
Not "Are you leaving?"
Not even "Are you right?"

They ask:

"Are you okay?"
"Are you tired?"
"Do you need anything?"

Elias answers honestly.

"No."
"No."
"No."

The absence of need confuses them.

One afternoon, a young man—new to the settlement, still learning its rhythms—asks him bluntly, "Why aren't you afraid?"

The question lands cleanly, without accusation.

Elias thinks for a moment.

"Because nothing is being taken from me," he says.

The young man frowns. "What about belonging?"

Elias smiles faintly. "Belonging isn't something they can remove."

The young man nods slowly, as if considering a thought he has never been allowed to finish.

That evening, Silas passes Elias near the inner lanes.

They do not stop.

"You're forcing our hand," Silas says quietly as they walk.

"I'm not," Elias replies just as quietly. "I'm removing yours."

Silas slows, but Elias does not.

"Authority cannot function without compliance," Silas says.

"Then it was never authority," Elias replies, not unkindly.

Silas stops walking.

Elias continues on, feeling no triumph—only sadness.

Later, Maren visits Elias at his home.

She sits across from him at the small table, hands wrapped around a cup she has not touched.

"They don't know what to do with you," she says.

"I know," Elias replies.

"They can't punish you without proving your point," she continues. "And they can't absorb you without changing."

Elias listens.

"They're hoping you'll compromise," Maren adds. "Offer something they can name."

Elias shakes his head. "Anything I offer becomes leverage."

Maren smiles, weary and relieved at once. "You've always understood power better than most."

"I don't think this is power," Elias says. "I think it's absence."

Maren's eyes soften. "Absence of fear," she says.

Elias nods.

They sit together in quiet for a while.

"You know," Maren says eventually, "they may decide you're unsafe simply because you can't be managed."

"I know," Elias replies.

"And you're staying anyway," she says.

"Yes."

Maren exhales, something like laughter in the sound. "That's infuriatingly consistent."

Elias smiles.

When she leaves, Elias stands by the window and watches the lamps flicker on across the lanes.

The rope near the markers remains slack.

Children pass beneath it without noticing.

Adults step around it carefully.

No one enforces it.

The absence of enforcement exposes the truth of it.

That night, Elias lies awake briefly, not with anxiety, but with awareness.

He understands now why fear is so useful.

It creates leverage.

It gives authority something to pull.

Remove fear, and authority must either transform—or reveal itself.

The settlement is at that threshold now.

Not because Elias has challenged it.

But because he has refused to give it anything to hold.

Whatever comes next will not be forced.

It will be chosen.

And that, Elias knows, is the most frightening—and freeing—condition of all.

Chapter 21 — Some Leave, Some Stay

The shift does not happen all at once.

It never does.

Instead, it arrives unevenly, like weather moving through a valley—one side in shadow, another already in light. The settlement begins to feel subtly out of sync with itself, as though different people are waking up in different seasons.

The first to leave do so quietly.

A family from the second ring packs their things over several days, speaking little of it. When asked, they say they have an opportunity elsewhere. The words are true enough. They do not mention unease, or the way the air has felt tighter lately, or how exhausting it has become to brace without knowing why.

Others follow, singly or in pairs.

Not in protest.

Not in anger.

Simply choosing space.

Their departures are polite. Orderly. Blessed, even. No one forbids them. No one names it as loss.

But absence accumulates.

Those who stay begin to notice.

Conversations circle more often around safety and continuity. Elders speak warmly of stability. The word *faithful* is used more frequently, as if loyalty itself requires reinforcement.

At the same time, something else is happening.

People begin lingering.

They stay longer after work. They sit together without agenda. They walk the inner lanes more slowly, not crossing lines, not testing rules—just inhabiting space without urgency.

Elias notices it everywhere.

At the well, a man admits quietly that he sleeps better lately.

Near the market, a woman laughs at herself for rushing and then doesn't correct it.

A child refuses to be hurried and is not scolded for it.

These people do not gather around Elias.

They simply move differently now.

Still, the division sharpens.

Those who leave speak of peace found elsewhere.

Those who stay speak of commitment.

Neither group is wrong.

But the language around staying begins to change.

It becomes heavier.

Maren names it one evening as they walk together near the third ring.

"They're confusing endurance with faithfulness," she says.

Elias nods. "Endurance needs fear."

"And faithfulness doesn't," Maren replies.

They stop where the lane curves inward, just before the markers.

"Silas believes those who leave are avoiding responsibility," Maren says.

"And those who stay?" Elias asks.

Maren exhales. "He believes they're proving something."

Elias looks toward the square.

"Proving what?" he asks.

"That fear is still necessary," Maren says quietly.

As the days pass, Elias feels no pull to convince either group.

Those who leave need no permission.

Those who stay need no argument.

What remains are the undecided—the ones who linger near thresholds, unsure which story to inhabit.

Authority watches them closely.

Not to punish.

To measure.

Elias understands now that systems are rarely threatened by rebellion.

They are threatened by choice.

One afternoon, Jonah appears again.

This time his shoulders are lighter.

"I think I'm staying," Jonah says.

Elias studies him. "Do you want to?"

Jonah hesitates. Then nods. "Yes. I think so."

"Not because you should?" Elias asks.

Jonah lets out a slow breath. "Not anymore."

They walk together for a while.

"Some of the people who left were my friends," Jonah says.

"I know," Elias replies.

"And some who stayed feel… brittle," Jonah adds.

"Yes," Elias says again.

Jonah glances at him. "You're not trying to replace anything, are you?"

Elias smiles faintly. "I wouldn't know how."

Jonah nods, satisfied.

As evening falls, the settlement feels quieter—not emptier, but more honest. The edges are clearer now. The strain of pretending unity where there is none has eased.

No one has won.

No one has lost.

But something essential has been revealed:

Belonging that depends on fear cannot survive choice.

Elias walks home beneath the lamps, listening to footsteps fade and reappear.

Some are leaving.

Some are staying.

And for the first time, neither feels like failure.

The centre remains where it always has been—unchanged, unpossessive, indifferent to outcome.

It does not ask anyone to stay.

It does not chase anyone who leaves.

It simply remains.

And in that remaining, Elias senses the beginning of something quieter and truer than unity:

Freedom.

Not enforced.

Not celebrated.

Just present.

Waiting to be lived.

Chapter 22 — Nearness

Elias waits until the settlement is quiet.

Not asleep—there are always lamps still burning, always someone awake with a child, a worry, a late task—but quiet in the way a place becomes quiet when it has stopped arguing with itself for a few hours.

The departures have slowed. The conversations have softened. The rope near the markers remains, slack and almost invisible in the dim light. No one enforces it now. No one needs to. People have either tightened their own boundaries or loosened them. Choice has done what instruction could not.

Elias has not crossed the markers since the slip.

Not because he is afraid.

Because he does not want the centre to become a symbol he uses. He does not want to turn it into a proof. He does not want to approach it in reaction to pressure, as if nearness is a stance rather than a reality.

But tonight, he finds himself standing at the edge of the inner lane with an unforced clarity.

Not urgency.

Not defiance.

A simple readiness—different from the settlement's idea of readiness, which requires permission and performance.

This readiness requires nothing.

He walks toward the markers slowly.

The air is cool and clean, carrying the faint scent of stone and damp earth. The lamps cast shallow pools of light, leaving long stretches of shadow between them. The inner lane feels wider at night, less crowded with expectation.

When he reaches the rope, he stops.

It hangs low between the posts, looped lazily, as if even the boundary is tired of its role. Elias looks at it for a moment—not with contempt, not with reverence.

Just seeing it for what it is.

A gesture.

He steps over it.

The movement is so ordinary it almost feels wrong. His boot clears the rope without brushing it. Nothing catches. Nothing resists. Nothing announces the crossing.

He is past the markers again.

He stands still and waits for his body to react.

For the tightening.

For the inner warning.

For the sense of being watched.

What comes instead is an almost imperceptible softening, like a muscle releasing after years of being held.

Elias lets out a slow breath.

The square lies ahead, pale in the dimness, the stones lighter here as if they carry their own quiet reflection. At the centre, the source rests as it always has—no glow, no movement, no spectacle. Just a dark pool held by worn stone.

It is smaller than fear made it.

He takes a few steps forward, then stops again.

He is close enough now that he can hear it.

Not a voice.

A sound.

Water, moving gently against stone.

The simplest sound in the world.

It strikes him, with a sudden tenderness, how much story has been built around something so ordinary.

He walks to the edge of the ring and crouches.

His hand hovers over the stone.

He remembers the way he wiped his hand on his coat last time, self-conscious, as if being seen touching stone could cost him something.

No one is here.

And yet the gesture still matters.

Not because anyone will witness it.

Because his body has been trained to treat nearness as trespass.

Elias places his hand on the ring.

The stone is cold.

It does not respond.

It does not grant.

It does not demand.

It simply remains.

Elias stays crouched for a long time.

He listens to the water.

He listens to his own breath.

He becomes aware, slowly, of how little he is thinking. Not because his mind is empty, but because it has stopped reaching for explanation.

There is no conclusion forming in him.

Only recognition.

He thinks of the settlement, of the way people have braced themselves their entire lives for a harm that never arrived. He thinks of Jonah's loyalty. Of Silas's careful words. Of Maren's weariness. Of children drawing circles in the dust, refusing to accept invisible lines as permanent.

He feels no resentment.

Only grief, soft and clean.

Grief for wasted vigilance.

Grief for love distorted into leverage.

Grief for the many ways people have learned to manage what was never fragile.

The grief rises, then settles.

It does not turn into accusation.

It simply passes through him like water through an opened channel.

Elias shifts closer and looks into the source.

The water is dark, reflecting only fragments of light. He can see his own face there—broken by ripple, softened by movement.

He does not look like someone receiving a revelation.

He looks like someone finally standing still.

Without thinking, Elias dips his fingers into the water.

The cold shocks him lightly, not unpleasant, just real.

He lifts his hand and lets the water fall back into the pool.

The ripples move outward in widening circles, touching the stone ring gently, then returning.

Nothing else happens.

No voice.

No sign.

No confirmation.

And yet Elias feels, with a certainty deeper than emotion, that this is the point.

Not spectacle.

Not proof.

Not punishment avoided.

Presence.

He sits back on his heels and closes his eyes.

In the darkness behind his eyelids, he senses the story he has lived under—the one that says nearness must be earned, that closeness requires readiness, that safety depends on fear.

He lets the story sit there for a moment, fully seen.

Then he lets it go.

Not with effort.

Not with drama.

It simply loosens, like a knot that has been held in place by tension rather than necessity.

Elias opens his eyes again.

The centre has not changed.

The settlement has not changed.

He has not become anyone new.

He has simply stopped bracing against what was never against him.

He stands slowly.

For a moment he remains at the edge of the source, looking outward to the rings, the lanes, the lamps. The settlement curves away from the centre like a thought that has been kept at a distance for too long.

He feels an unexpected tenderness toward it.

Not as a system.

As people.

He understands then that the centre was never meant to be possessed.

It was never meant to be guarded.

It was meant to be trusted.

Elias turns and walks back toward the markers.

When he steps over the rope again, he does it without contempt. He does not kick it aside. He does not untie it. He leaves it where it hangs, because moving it would make it a statement.

He is not making statements.

He is living.

As he reaches the inner lane, he hears footsteps behind him.

He stops.

A figure stands near the marker line, half in shadow, half in lamplight.

Maren.

She is not surprised to see him.

"I thought you might come," she says quietly.

Elias's throat tightens. "I didn't plan it."

Maren nods. "That's why I knew."

They stand together for a moment, the rope between them and the square barely visible.

"What did you find?" Maren asks.

143

Elias considers the question.

"I found," he says slowly, "that nothing was waiting to hurt me."

Maren's eyes close briefly. When she opens them, they shine with something that might be relief.

"And the rest?" she asks.

Elias looks toward the square, then back to her.

"The rest," he says, "was already here."

Maren exhales, a sound like surrender.

They do not speak again.

They walk back toward the third ring side by side, unhurried.

Behind them, the centre remains what it has always been.

The place that never left.

Still there.

Not calling.

Not chasing.

Not withholding.

Only present—quietly undoing fear by refusing to participate in it at all.

Chapter 23 — Re-Seeing

In the days that follow, no announcement is made.

There is no gathering where Silas stands and revises the story. No elder confesses fear. No one declares a new season for the settlement.

Change does not arrive as proclamation.

It arrives as permission.

It begins in small ways that are almost impossible to track.

A parent lets a child linger nearer the inner lanes without yanking them back.

A worker takes the shorter route instead of the safer one, and does not apologise.

Someone steps over the slack rope without noticing they've done it, then pauses, then keeps walking.

Nothing breaks.

Nothing happens.

The settlement absorbs these moments the way stone absorbs warmth—slowly, invisibly, until one day you realise the cold has lifted.

Elias says very little.

He continues his work. He repairs what needs repair. He speaks when spoken to. He answers questions plainly, without framing. He refuses to become the centre of a movement.

That refusal becomes part of the re-seeing.

People had expected a leader.

A teacher.

A rebel.

Instead they find a man who is simply no longer afraid.

And because he is not trying to persuade them, they begin to notice their own fear without defensiveness.

One afternoon, a woman stops Elias near the well.

"I stepped over it," she says, voice low, as if confessing.

Elias looks at her. "Over what?"

She glances toward the inner lanes. "The rope."

Elias nods. "Alright."

She frowns, unsettled by the lack of reaction.

"I thought I'd feel something," she says. "Guilt. Fear. Something."

"And?" Elias asks.

"Nothing," she admits. "Just… space."

Elias nods again. "Then that's what was there."

She looks at him for a moment longer, as if waiting for instruction, then turns and walks away, shoulders slightly lower than when she arrived.

Another day, Jonah finds Elias near the market stalls.

Jonah looks tired, but not brittle now—tired in the way someone is tired after finally seeing what they've been carrying.

"I used to think fear was the proof that I cared," Jonah says quietly.

Elias waits.

"And now?" Elias asks.

Jonah swallows. "Now I think fear was the thing stopping me from trusting what I said I believed."

Elias does not correct him.

He does not affirm him loudly either.

He simply nods, letting Jonah's words settle where they belong.

Not as doctrine.

As discovery.

Not everyone re-sees.

Some still avoid the inner lanes entirely, doubling down on distance with quiet conviction. They speak of wisdom and boundaries and the dangers of looseness. They are not cruel.

They are frightened.

Elias understands that fear, once it has been called safety, resists being named.

But even among those who remain afraid, the tone begins to shift. The edge of certainty softens. The need to correct others lessens.

Without leverage, fear loses its sharpness.

It can no longer prove itself by enforcement.

It must either be released—or carried honestly.

The elders respond unevenly.

The older woman who had spoken of responsibility begins to walk the inner lanes more often, saying little, watching everything. She does not retract her previous stance. She simply inhabits the space with new attentiveness, as if gathering evidence she never allowed herself to seek.

The practical elder continues speaking of safety, but with less insistence. He stops watching the rope. He stops hovering near the markers. He begins, without admitting it, to let people choose.

Silas is the one who struggles most.

Not because he is evil, and not even because he is afraid of the centre.

Because he is afraid of what the centre makes unnecessary.

He speaks less in gatherings now. When he does speak, his words are careful but slightly hollow, as if he can feel the settlement no longer needing interpretation in the same way.

One evening, Elias finds Silas alone near the records room.

Silas looks up when he sees him, expression composed.

"You've been quiet," Silas says.

"So have you," Elias replies.

Silas's mouth tightens faintly. "The settlement is changing."

Elias nods. "Yes."

Silas watches him for a moment.

"You know," Silas says, "there are reasons we built what we built."

Elias believes him.

"I know," he says.

"And you're letting it loosen anyway," Silas adds.

Elias meets his gaze. "I'm not loosening it," he says. "I'm refusing to tighten it."

Silas exhales.

"That distinction feels… convenient," he says.

"It's honest," Elias replies.

Silas looks away, eyes settling on the shelves, the accumulated story of years.

"People need language," he says quietly. "They need meaning."

Elias nods. "Yes."

"And if they don't receive meaning from us," Silas continues, "they will make their own."

Elias's voice is gentle.

"Maybe that's what you're afraid of," he says.

Silas looks back at him, something like pain flickering behind his composure.

"I'm afraid of chaos," Silas says.

Elias hears the sincerity.

"Then watch," Elias replies. "There hasn't been chaos. Only choice."

Silas holds his gaze for a long moment, then looks down.

"It won't always be so clean," he murmurs.

"No," Elias agrees. "But fear isn't cleanliness. It's control."

Silas does not answer.

Elias turns and leaves him with the thought.

In the weeks that follow, the rope becomes irrelevant.

Not removed.

Just forgotten.

It still hangs slack between the posts, weathered by rain and sun, a relic of an attempt to clarify something that never needed clarifying.

Children play near it. Adults step around it or over it without comment.

The markers remain, but their meaning changes.

They become less a warning and more a memory.

The centre stays the same.

The water continues its quiet movement against stone.

No power is displayed.

No proof is given.

And that, slowly, becomes the proof.

People begin to speak differently, not in gatherings, but in doorways and lanes and small moments.

"I always thought…"
"I never realised…"

"It wasn't what they said…"
"It was never gone…"

They do not say, "We were wrong."

They say, "We didn't see."

Re-seeing is gentler than repentance as they had once been taught.

It carries less shame.

More breath.

Elias notices, one evening, that he is no longer watching the settlement for reaction.

He is simply living in it.

He walks the lanes without calculating distance. He steps nearer the centre sometimes, not making a pilgrimage, not chasing a feeling—just letting his body exist where fear once forbade it.

He does not become special.

He becomes ordinary.

And ordinariness, he realises, is what fear-based stories always stole first.

Not salvation.

Not holiness.

Simple life.

The settlement does not become perfect.

It becomes less braced.

Some leave.

Some stay.

Some re-see.

Some resist.

But the centre remains what it has always been—quiet, present, unpossessive.

The place that never left.

And in the slow, uneven unfolding of new permission, the settlement begins to learn what no one can be forced into:

When the story changes, the centre does not.

Only the eyes that finally dare to look.

Chapter 24 — The Place That Never Left

Morning comes the way it always has.

Light spreads slowly across stone. Doors open. Water is drawn. Bread is broken. The settlement wakes without announcement, without urgency, without the sense that something must be decided today.

Elias walks early, as he often does now.

He does not check where he is allowed to go.

He does not measure distance.

He simply walks.

The inner lanes feel familiar in a way they never did before—not because they have changed, but because he has stopped approaching them as territory that requires negotiation. The stones are worn where feet have always passed. The curves are gentle. Nothing here is dramatic.

He reaches the square while it is still empty.

The rope is gone.

Not removed ceremonially. Not cut. Not discussed.

Simply absent.

The posts remain, pale lines catching the morning light, but whatever was looped between them has been untied and carried away without comment.

Elias pauses, surprised by the quietness of the moment.

He expected something to register.

Nothing does.

He walks into the square and sits on the edge of the stone ring, as he has done before. The water reflects the sky in broken pieces, moving gently, endlessly.

It is the same.

He rests his hands on the stone and feels its cold solidity beneath his palms.

No permission was asked.

No boundary was crossed.

This is what was always here.

Footsteps sound behind him.

He turns to see Lio approaching, walking with the unselfconscious confidence of a child who has never learned to perform hesitation.

"You came early," the boy says.

"So did you," Elias replies.

Lio shrugs. "I like it quiet."

They sit together, legs dangling, watching the water.

"Did you know," Lio says, "that some people thought it was dangerous?"

Elias smiles faintly. "I did."

Lio frowns. "It doesn't look dangerous."

"It isn't," Elias says.

Lio nods, satisfied.

After a moment, he asks, "Why did they say it was?"

Elias considers how much to say.

"Because they were afraid," he says gently.

"Of the water?" Lio asks.

Elias shakes his head. "Of being close."

Lio thinks about this.

"That's silly," he says.

Elias laughs softly. "Sometimes."

They sit in companionable silence.

As the morning deepens, others begin to arrive—not gathering, not assembling, just passing through the square on their way elsewhere. Some pause. Some don't. A few sit for a moment, then move on.

No one guards the space.

No one explains it.

It is simply used.

Maren passes through midmorning. She catches Elias's eye and nods once, a small, wordless acknowledgment. She does not stop.

She does not need to.

Silas does not come.

Elias notices this without judgment.

Some things take longer.

By midday, the square is alive with ordinary movement. Children run across it without slowing. Adults cross the stone ring on their way to other places, stepping close to the water without noticing the significance of what they are doing.

The centre has become what it always was.

A centre.

Not a test.

Not a reward.

Not a threat.

Elias watches this without satisfaction.

He feels no sense of victory.

Only a quiet gratitude that nothing needed to be defended for it to remain true.

Later, as the day stretches and softens, Elias leaves the square and walks the outer lanes again. He repairs a loose stone. He helps lift a cart. He shares bread with someone who sits beside him without explanation.

Life continues.

That evening, as the lamps are lit and the settlement settles into its familiar rhythms, Elias walks home and sits by the window one last time.

The square is visible from here, dimly lit, unremarkable.

He realises something then, not as insight but as release:

He no longer watches the centre to see what it will do.

He no longer watches the settlement to see what it will decide.

He no longer watches himself to see if he is allowed to be here.

The watching has ended.

Trust has taken its place.

Not trust in systems.

Not trust in leaders.

Not even trust in outcomes.

Trust in presence.

Trust that what is real does not withdraw when fear releases its grip.

Trust that closeness was never the reward for readiness, but the ground beneath it.

Elias closes the window and prepares for sleep.

Tomorrow will come.

People will choose differently.

Some will still fear.

Some will still leave.

Some will still stay.

None of that will change what has already been true.

The place did not return.

It did not open.

It did not become safe.

It never left.

And neither, Elias knows now, did he.

www.ingramcontent.com/pod-product-compliance
Lightning Source LLC
Chambersburg PA
CBHW050856180626
46814CB00007B/2763